OXFORD WORLD

CASTLE RA

Maria Edgeworth was born in Oxfordshire in 1767 or 1768. On her father's second marriage in 1773, she went with him to Ireland. Her father employed her in keeping accounts and in dealing with his tenants. She also acquired a familiarity with fashionable people, and with Irish peasantry, all of which was to be of use in her novels. Her father made her a confidential friend, and he also became her literary adviser. Much of her early writing was for children, and it was not until 1800 that she appeared as a novelist for adult readers with the publication of *Castle Rackrent*. Its vigorous descriptions of Irish characters made the book an instant success. In 1798 the marriage of her father to his fourth wife brought her an intimate friend for fifty-one years in her new stepmother. Maria Edgeworth showed great business talent, and took a keen personal interest in the poor upon the estate. She was of diminutive stature, with a vivacious and amiable character. After some years of illness she died in the arms of her stepmother on 22 May 1849.

Kathryn J. Kirkpatrick, who provided the Introduction and Bibliography for this edition, is Associate Professor of English at Appalachian State University. She has also edited Edgeworth's *Belinda* and Susan Ferrier's *Marriage*, for Oxford World's Classics.

George Watson, the textual editor of this volume, is Fellow in English of St John's College, Cambridge. His publications include *The Story of the Novel* (1979).

OXFORD WORLD'S CLASSICS

For over 100 years Oxford World's Classics have brought readers closer to the world's great literature. Now with over 700 titles—from the 4,000-year-old myths of Mesopotamia to the twentieth century's greatest novels—the series makes available lesser-known as well as celebrated writing.

The pocket-sized hardbacks of the early years contained introductions by Virginia Woolf, T. S. Eliot, Graham Greene, and other literary figures which enriched the experience of reading. Today the series is recognized for its fine scholarship and reliability in texts that span world literature, drama and poetry, religion, philosophy and politics. Each edition includes perceptive commentary and essential background information to meet the changing needs of readers.

OXFORD WORLD'S CLASSICS

MARIA EDGEWORTH

Castle Rackrent

Edited by

GEORGE WATSON

With an Introduction by

KATHRYN J. KIRKPATRICK

OXFORD
UNIVERSITY PRESS

Great Clarendon Street, Oxford OX2 6DP

Oxford University Press is a department of the University of Oxford.
It furthers the University's objective of excellence in research, scholarship,
and education by publishing worldwide in

Oxford New York

Athens Auckland Bangkok Bogotá Buenos Aires Calcutta
Cape Town Chennai Dar es Salaam Delhi Florence Hong Kong Istanbul
Karachi Kuala Lumpur Madrid Melbourne Mexico City Mumbai
Nairobi Paris São Paulo Singapore Taipei Tokyo Toronto Warsaw
with associated companies in Berlin Ibadan

Oxford is a registered trade mark of Oxford University Press
in the UK and in certain other countries

Published in the United States
by Oxford University Press Inc., New York

First published by Oxford University Press 1964
This edition, with new Introduction and Bibliography,
first published as a World's Classics paperback 1995
Reissued as an Oxford World's Classics paperback 1999
Reissued 2008

British Library Cataloguing in Publication Data
Data available

Library of Congress Cataloging in Publication Data
Edgeworth, Maria, 1767–1849.
Caslte Rackrent / Maria Edgeworth ; edited by George Watson ; with
an introduction by Kathryn J. Kirkpatrick.
p. cm.—(Oxford world's classics)
Includes bibliographical references
1. Ireland—Social life and customs—19th century—Fiction.
2. Administration of estates—Ireland—Fiction. I. Watson, George,
1927– . II. Title. III. Series.
PR4644C3 1995 823'.7—dc20 94–48873

ISBN 978–0–19–953755–6

15

Printed and bound in Great Britain by
Clays Ltd, Elcograf S.p.A.

CONTENTS

INTRODUCTION

Castle Rackrent (1800) may well be one of the most famous unread novels in English. Innovative, prophetic, and artistically masterful, the book both borrows from and originates a variety of literary genres and subgenres without fitting neatly into any of them. This protean quality may account for the novel's ambiguous status in the literary canon as well as its pervasive influence. Combining the subtle wit of the French tale, the Gaelic cadences of Irish oral tradition, and Gothic intrigue over property and inheritance, *Castle Rackrent* has gathered a dazzling array of firsts—the first regional novel, the first socio-historical novel, the first Irish novel, the first Big House novel, the first saga novel. This achievement echoes in the praise of other writers. Sir Walter Scott acknowledged his great debt to Edgeworth's 'admirable Irish portraits' in his postscript to *Waverley* (1814). Later in the century, the Irish writer Emily Lawless claimed Maria Edgeworth as her literary mother and produced in her short story, 'Mrs O'Donnell's Report', a female counterpart to the *Rackrent* narrator, Thady Quirk. William Butler Yeats was unstinting in his praise, calling *Castle Rackrent* 'one of the most inspired chronicles written in English'.[1] Indeed,

[1] W. B. Yeats, *Representative Irish Tales* (1891; Atlantic Highlands, NJ, 1979), 27.

the novel's rambling plot, attention to narrative voice, and ruined Anglo-Irish house have become staples of Irish fiction, appearing variously in the work of Charles Lever and Somerville and Ross in the nineteenth century, and James Joyce, Elizabeth Bowen, and, most recently, Jennifer Johnson and John Banville in the twentieth century. If, as David Richter has argued, neglected novels receive attention 'when the literary horizon has, in effect, caught up with them',[2] then surely, for *Castle Rackrent*, the moment has arrived.

More accurately, it has returned: *Castle Rackrent* was widely read in its own day. On a visit to England in 1802 Richard Lovell Edgeworth enquired after his daughter's burgeoning canon at a circulating library and found *Belinda* (1801) and *Essay on Irish Bulls* (1802) 'often borrowed, but "Castle Rackrent" often bought'.[3] With the publication of the second edition in 1801, *Castle Rackrent*'s popularity was so great that others claimed authorship of the anonymously published volume, one covetous author even copying out pages and inserting corrections to make his manuscript appear original.[4] Writing to the English clergyman Dr Beaufort, Richard Edgeworth recorded the response of George III: 'We hear from good authority that the

[2] David Richter, 'The Reception of the Gothic Novel in the 1790s', in Robert W. Uphaus (ed.), *The Idea of the Novel in the Eighteenth Century* (East Lansing, MI, 1988), 118.

[3] ME to Miss Sneyd, 27 Sept. 1802; quoted in Augustus Hare (ed.), *Life and Letters of Maria Edgeworth* (1894; Freeport, NY, 1971), i. 87.

[4] Ibid. 76.

King was much pleased with Castle Rackrent—he rubbed his hands and said what—what—I know something now of my Irish subjects.'[5] But what encouraged the Edgeworths more was the novel's favourable reception among the Anglo-Irish themselves. They had not believed its portrait of feckless landlords would please the gentry in Ireland. Indeed, hints of displeasure did appear in 1803 when an anonymous letter arrived at Edgeworthstown 'enclosing a page of Castle Rackrent on which was scrawled lies, lies, lies in pencil'.[6]

Maria Edgeworth had tried to avoid the censure of the Anglo-Irish by setting her satiric portrait of them in the past, 'before the year 1782'. In her Preface, she urged her readers to observe 'that the manners depicted in the following pages are not those of the present age' (p. 4). But it was a distinction lost on some, perhaps in part because the abuses she reported in her novel, rack-renting and absenteeism, still so afflicted and riled Irish Catholics that they struck back at the Anglo-Irish gentry through rural protest. Though a member of the landowning class, Maria Edgeworth was not uncritical of its exploitative practices. In *Castle Rackrent* she adopts the voice of an outsider to satirize the Anglo-Irish gentry. Indeed, the situation of her Irish Catholic narrator, Thady Quirk,

[5] RLE to D. A. Beaufort, 26 Apr. 1800 (National Library of Ireland, MS 10166).

[6] Charlotte Edgeworth to Emmeline King, 25 Sept. 1803 (National Library of Ireland, MS 10166).

a man of divided loyalties and limited power, parallels her own ambiguous status as a woman of the Big House, similarly subordinate, without property or political franchise. These overlapping identities, narrated in a context of political crisis, give *Castle Rackrent* its hybridized, complex form. Written during the turbulent 1790s—the decade of the Defenders and the United Irishmen—and published on the eve of the Union, the novel can be read as an important document in the tortuous struggle for Irish national identity, a struggle Edgeworth must have felt on some level as her own. Far from the propaganda that some have accused Edgeworth of producing for her own class, *Castle Rackrent* takes up the issue of Protestant legitimacy in Ireland at precisely the moment when it was facing a most serious challenge. The very title of the novel, by evoking both the castle as embodiment of hereditary right to land as well as the system of rackrenting which abused that power, begins the novel's interrogation of property relations in Ireland.

It is significant that Maria Edgeworth chose *The Black Book of Edgeworthstown*, a chronicle of her own family's struggles to secure its Irish estate, as a source for *Castle Rackrent*. Written by her grandfather during the middle of the eighteenth century, *The Black Book* is part family history, part ledger and litigation record. It relates the efforts of Richard Edgeworth (senior) to rid the estate of generations of accumulated debt and to settle in court various claims to the land. Embedded within the pages of legal and financial detail is a record of lineage—thirty-eight pages of memoirs documenting the family's history from its arrival in Ireland.

The Edgeworth property—almost 600 acres near Mastrim, County Longford—had been granted to Francis Edgeworth in 1619 as part of James I's decision to settle Protestants of English descent on land confiscated from Irish Catholics. It was a policy which, along with the Penal Laws, sought to sever Catholics from their property, their educational institutions, and their religious practices while giving political control of Ireland to the Protestant settlers. Roman Catholics were denied the vote and excluded from the Irish Parliament. By the late eighteenth century the property laws had done their work: out of a total population of four million in Ireland, 5,000 Protestant families possessed 95 per cent of the land.[7]

Yet, as the Edgeworth ledgers suggest, the control of Ireland by the Anglo-Irish was never secure. In the Catholic rebellion of 1642, Maria Edgeworth's great-great-grandmother had been among those who fled to England while Cromwell harshly subdued the rebels. On this occasion the Edgeworth estate just missed being burned to the ground. It was saved by a servant who urged that the house be spared because among its residents had been Jane Tuite, a practising Catholic

[7] J. H. Andrews, 'Land and People, *c.*1780', in T. W. Moody and W. E. Vaughan (eds.), *Eighteenth-Century Ireland, 1691–1800* (*Oxford*, 1986), 237.

and the third wife of Francis Edgeworth. Seeing her portrait in the hall, the rebels agreed to leave the estate.[8]

A similar connection with the Catholic community protected the Edgeworth estate during the rebellion of 1798. In this instance, one of the rebel leaders recalled that the Edgeworth housekeeper had 'the year before, lent his wife, when in distress, sixteen shillings, the rent of flax-ground'. In gratitude, the rebel reassured the housekeeper 'that no harm should happen to her or any belonging to her; not a soul should get leave to go into her master's house: not a twig should be touched, nor a leaf harmed'.[9] Customary bonds between Irish Catholics saved the Edgeworths on both occasions.

On one level, *Castle Rackrent* explores the social consequences of the displacement of these ancient Catholic customs by a Protestant-enacted rule of law. Moving from a common tradition to written law, Ireland was, under Protestant rule, following England, where a Parliament controlled by landowners enacted enclosures of common lands held under long-standing tenants' rights. In both countries ancient customs were being displaced by the *laissez-faire* practices of agrarian capitalists, and for the rising classes, proficiency in law became a key to economic success. Maria Edgeworth's

[8] Harriet Jessie Butler and Harold Edgeworth Butler (eds.), *The Black Book of Edgeworthstown and Other Edgeworth Memories, 1585–1817* (London, 1927), 12.

[9] Grace Oliver, *A Study of Maria Edgeworth with Notices of Her Father and Friends* (Boston, 1882), 118.

father trained as a lawyer and she herself recommended such an education for men in her novels *Ennui* (1809) and *Patronage* (1814). Indeed, Edgeworth's early educational works articulated the more liberatory aspects of the new capitalist culture: individual worth sprang from personal merit, and education and exertion ideally made advancement possible for anyone, regardless of family tradition or lineage. But she was not blind to the disruptive excesses this philosophy could produce in traditional cultures. In *Castle Rackrent* she satirized the misuse of power in both systems—the feudal oppression of Catholic custom and the ruthless greed of Protestant law.

The Black Book's portraits of Maria Edgeworth's Anglo-Irish ancestors gave her a wealth of material. In a letter of 1834 she wrote that the 'good-natured and indolent extravagance' of Sir Condy in *Castle Rackrent* was 'suggested by a relation of mine long since dead'.[10] Indeed, a kind of reckless colonial plunder marks the lives of many of the early Edgeworths. One sold land to buy expensive clothes, including a 'high-crowned beaver hat'. Another amassed huge gambling debts and forced his eldest son to mortgage his house to pay them. Younger brothers took an older brother to court to squabble over land, and a mother and sister insisted on their right to a portion of the Edgeworth

[10] ME to Mrs Stark, 6 Sept. 1834; quoted in Frances Edgeworth, *A Memoir of Maria Edgeworth, with a Selection from Her Letters*, iii. (London, 1867), 153.

property. What *The Black Book* reveals is that Protestant rule of law, particularly primogeniture, found rocky ground in Ireland. Even to Protestants themselves the new legalism looked like arbitrary land-grabbing. Women and younger sons in the Edgeworth family responded by challenging the eldest son's hold on his Irish property. Yet, without this heir and the stability of the legal system of primogeniture that he represented, the entire English presence in Ireland had no foundation. It thus became one of the projects of Maria Edgeworth in her Irish fiction to reconstruct this Anglo-Irish heir; he had to be remade in an image worthy of the legitimacy he sought in Ireland. If he could not govern his own estate successfully, he could not hope to play an effective role in governing the country as a whole. Indeed, these were views her immediate family had already embraced and acted upon.

Many landlords and their families in Ireland in the late eighteenth century were absentees; even those who were not, rarely involved themselves directly in the management of the land. Most relied on a middleman who, as Edgeworth maintains in her continuation of *The Black Book*, 'took the land at a reasonable rent and sub-let at the highest price he could get, a procedure which caused untold misery'.[11] This 'rack-renting' also appalled English improvers like Arthur Young:

[11] Butler and Butler, *The Black Book of Edgeworthstown*, 157–8.

Living upon the spot, surrounded by their little under-tenants, they [middlemen] prove the most oppressive species of tyrant that ever lent assistance to the destruction of a country. They re-let the land, at short tenures, to occupiers of small farms; and often give no leases at all. Not satisfied with screwing up the rent to the uttermost farthing, they are rapacious and relentless in the collection of it.[12]

Because the middleman was responsible for nothing more than providing the highest sum to his employer and himself by whatever means available, he represented the worst excesses of agrarian capitalism. Yet the system, in the long run, was not even particularly profitable. It led to overworked land, haphazard farming practices, and run-down cottages.

When Maria Edgeworth's father arrived from England with his family in 1782, he radically altered estate management at Edgeworthstown. Combining some of the principles of the English capitalist improvers with an old-fashioned paternalism, he removed many of the middleman's excesses. Unlike some of his English counterparts, he did not rely on landless labourers who were forced to work for the lowest wage. Yet he also erased elements of custom—some of which favoured the landlord, such as duty fowl and duty work, and some of which favoured the tenant, such as seniority in tenure and partnership farming. These changes restored reciprocity and social responsibility to

[12] Arthur Hutton (ed.), *Arthur Young's Tour in Ireland, 1776–1779* (London, 1892), 26.

relations that, through absenteeism and middlemen, had too often been allowed to degenerate exclusively into self-interest and profit-making.

Maria Edgeworth's personal experience was thus unusual on two counts. First, she belonged to an Anglo-Irish family that lived on and worked its Irish property rather than following the more usual practice of draining the estate of rents. Secondly, her status within the family was uncommon for the time: as a young woman she assisted her father in estate management and became thoroughly familiar with the improvements he sought to make as well as with the Irish Catholic tenantry.[13] Given this context, it becomes even more clear why Maria Edgeworth chose to satirize the Anglo-Irish legacy she found in *The Black Book*. Her grandfather had himself disapproved of these ancestors and he had spent his life repairing the consequences of their excesses. Maria Edgeworth understandably wished to ally herself with the progressive course her family was now charting.

With its collection of inept landlords, *Castle Rackrent* elaborates the lessons of *The Black Book* by demonstrating all the ways that estate management in Ireland could go wrong. We are told in the novel's opening pages that Sir Patrick O'Shaughlin inherits the Rackrent estate from a first cousin, Sir Tallyhoo Rackrent, who died in a hunting accident caused by his

[13] Marilyn Butler, *Maria Edgeworth: A Literary Biography* (Oxford, 1972), 88.

refusal to put gates on his roads—he is the novel's first example of a landowner whose own neglect is eventually visited on himself. O'Shaughlin comes to ruin in another way. Heir to the income of a new exploitative system, he cannot see his way clear to embrace, reform, or reject it. He thus lives out his ambivalence by maintaining his social connections with a Catholic community in a way that quite literally mortgages the future of his estate.[14] Sir Patrick's lavish entertaining both endears him to the community and leaves him open to having his body claimed by creditors at his own funeral. When the lower ranks of Catholics, acting on customary loyalty, attempt to rescue his body, they fail, for the seizure is a sham staged by his son in order to rid himself of his father's debts. Communal and family feeling are usurped by economic self-interest.

This second-generation Rackrent heir is a litigating fiend: 'every thing upon the face of the earth furnished him with good matter for a suit. He used to boast that he had a law-suit for every letter in the alphabet' (p. 15). Sir Murtagh's passion for court cases is so excessive that he sells land in order to carry on suits and thereby defeats his own purposes. Yet despite his apparent devotion to

[14] Although his religion is never mentioned directly, it is clear that O'Shaughlin is Catholic: his name, we are told, is from an old family 'related to the Kings of Ireland'. His *change* of name, as a requirement for owning property, may also represent a change of creed. Under the Penal Laws, Catholics were required to convert to Protestantism and the Established Church in order to retain possession of their landed property.

litigation for its own sake, Murtagh also insists on retaining those elements of custom which serve his own interests. His estate management is based on a thoroughgoing exploitation of his tenants. Although Murtagh insists on prompt payment (contrary to customary practice), when it comes to duty work, he not only supports custom but uses his knowledge of law to put teeth into its enforcement, through 'strict clauses with heavy penalties'. Yet perhaps Sir Murtagh's most blatant abuse of law appears in the reverse poaching he carries out on his tenants. By failing to maintain his property and keep his fences mended, he marks himself as a landlord with little interest in improvement. However, by invoking trespass laws to seize his tenant's property, he makes use of a legal structure designed precisely to protect enclosed or improved land. He has, in effect, acted on laws of enclosure without having done the enclosing. The practice is emblematic of the profound lack of reciprocity involved in Sir Murtagh's estate management.

The next Rackrent heir, Sir Murtagh's younger brother, Sir Kit Stopgap, is a classic example of the absentee landlord: he stays at the Rackrent estate during the hunting season and spends the rest of his time in England, mostly in Bath, where he gambles. The estate's management falls to the notorious figure of the middleman whose sole concern is immediate profit. Customary rights of tenants are, in this generation, wholly ignored. Rents must be paid up to the day and farms at the end of leases are advertised to the highest bidder, 'all the old tenants turned out, when they had spent their substance in the hope and trust of a renewal from the landlord' (p. 21). Here Edgeworth represents the abuse of litigation as a profoundly negative relation to the land. Only after he imprisons his wife does Sir Kit become less marginal in the community. He holds large dinners and in a mock display drinks his lady's health at each occasion. But a sense of community can only be mimicked by this Rackrent heir; just as his relations with his wife are exploitative, oppressive, and ultimately grounded on brute force, so are his relations with the community. For the Rackrent neighbours, the narrator tells us, fail to challenge the imprisonment of Lady Rackrent because they fear Sir Kit: he has the reputation of being a good shot in a duel. Finally, in this portrayal of the ascendancy of rule of law, lawlessness prevails. Having lived by the duel, Sir Kit dies by one. Lady Rackrent gains her freedom and returns to England to live on her own income, an income her husband never succeeded in possessing.

That the Rackrent wives should prosper in the face of their husbands' ruin creates an interesting contradiction for the project which Maria Edgeworth had set herself in the first part of the novel. In reconstructing an heir worthy of Irish legitimacy, Edgeworth was, as a woman, fortifying a system of primogeniture which separated women from access to property. Her ambivalence works itself out in *Castle Rackrent* through the negative examples of landlords; while their satiric treatment is in the service of a more responsible landlordism, the *effect* of their portrayal is to kill off the patriarchs in the narrative, which results in increased prosperity for the novel's women.

This conflict between class alliance and gender equality, a conflict which threatened class stability, was active in Edgeworth's own life. At this point *Castle Rackrent* directs us outward to the context of its composition, the political rebellion of 1798 in Ireland, during which Maria Edgeworth saw her own Protestant class seriously threatened. At the same time, she came into her own as a writer.

As early as 1792 Maria Edgeworth wrote to her aunt of her wish 'that all the black clouds in the political horizon' would disperse, and two years later she relayed news of a Defender raid on a house half a mile from Edgeworthstown.[15] By January 1796 she was resorting to the droll tone that became characteristic in her descriptions of immediate personal danger during the Irish rebellion. 'All that I crave for my own part is, that if I am to have my throat cut, it may not be by a man with his face blackened by charcoal.'[16]

These letters reflect the escalating rural violence in Ireland during the 1790s as the Irish poor—the Defen-

[15] ME to Mrs Ruxton, 13 Dec. 1792 and 11 Aug. 1794; quoted in Hare, *Life and Letters*, i. 30, 38.

[16] ME to Mrs Ruxton, Jan. 1796; quoted ibid. 44.

ders—struck out at English Protestant settlers. Scores of Protestants were murdered and mutilated, and the retaliation of the Anglo-Irish government was no less grim: they quartered and disembowelled Catholics, and stuck their heads on spikes. This impasse found further expression in the conflict between the Orange Order and the Society of United Irishmen. Supporting the newly coined Phrase, 'Protestant ascendancy', members of the Orange Order argued that the task of the government was to ensure Protestant control of the country. Catholics and liberal Protestants countered with the formation of the United Irishmen in 1791, an organization which increasingly turned from stalled reform efforts to plans for alliance with France and the overthrow of the Anglo-Irish government by direct action in favour of an Irish republic.

From within this political maelstrom, Richard Edgeworth articulated the stakes with surprising lucidity. Writing to his sister Margaret Ruxton on 13 December 1792, he avowed:

the preservation of my Estate shall never be my Criterion of the part I should take in Politics—My firm persuasion that the Catholics *should* be represented numerically and without relation to property is certainly adverse to my own interest possessed as I am now of landed property by the right of Conquest—That right has hitherto been sufficient for the common purposes and common sense of mankind—Upon what foundation is another question... It is my dear Sister my firm belief that the Catholics must from the present state of European Politics necessarily obtain an entire participation of all the functions of Citizens.[17]

Here, in a single paragraph, Richard Edgeworth calls into question the very claim to Protestant legitimacy in Ireland which his father had been at such pains, over a lifetime, to construct. As a supporter of the American and French revolutions, Richard Edgeworth was eager to argue from enlightened principle rather than material self-interest. Yet, in this letter, he also acknowledges that his views are not particularly consistent with maintaining his position as a landowner. He had, in effect, articulated the politics of the United Irishmen from a material base which the Orange Order was desperate to defend.

This stance had dangerous consequences for the Edgeworths during the rebellion of 1798 when Ireland faced invasion by a French army sent to aid Irish insurgents. Long a vocal proponent of Catholic relief, Richard Edgeworth was not much admired by the Orangemen who ran County Longford. When he raised a militia from both Catholic and Protestant tenants to defend his estate, he was suspected by his Protestant landowning neighbours of being a rebel himself. Forced to leave the estate house after reports of approaching rebels, the Edgeworths made their way to town, where Richard Edgeworth was attacked by a crowd who accused him of being a traitor and a spy for

[17] RLE to Mrs Ruxton, 13 Dec. 1792; quoted in Butler, *Maria Edgeworth*, 112.

the French; he had to be rescued by English soldiers. Even after the French invasion had been thwarted and the Edgeworths were safely home, the rumours among Protestants continued. Every house in the surrounding countryside had been broken into and plundered except the Edgeworth estate house, and stories continued to circulate about Edgeworth's possible role in the conspiracy.

Maria Edgeworth felt the political and social dislocation of these years deeply. Only months before the rebellion, she had written to her cousin that 'a religious war in Ireland must be worse than any other' and her desire for the prosperity of peace embraced all factions: 'all we wish is to see everybody as happy as ourselves.'[18] Like her Quaker contemporary, Mary Leadbeater, Edgeworth was appalled by the brutality of her Protestant neighbours. These men, who saw 'all things with an orange jaundiced eye', had, she learned, planned her father's assassination during the family's flight to Longford, first intending to 'throw him into the river . . . then tie him upon his own grey horse, lead him through the streets of Longford with a pike stuck through his hand and at last to shoot him'.[19] But she was shocked too by the behaviour of those Irish Catholics she had considered loyal. Some had joined

[18] ME to Sophy Ruxton, 20 June 1798 (National Library of Ireland, MS 10166).

[19] ME to Sophy Ruxton, 19 Sept. 1798 (National Library of Ireland, MS 10166).

the rebels, planning to divide among themselves the Edgeworth lands and house. This encounter with the multiple betrayals made possible by the colonial system took its toll. 'I feel', she wrote in late September, 'as if I should be at once cowardly and suspicious for the rest of my life.'[20]

The structure of *Castle Rackrent* was moulded by this fraught context. Begun in the mid-1790s as a private entertainment, the novel took its 'voice', quite literally, from the family steward, John Langan, whom Edgeworth became proficient at imitating, claiming that she could think and speak in his dialect without effort. Hearing her impressions of Langan, Edgeworth's Aunt Ruxton urged her to develop a tale, and Edgeworth wrote the first half of *Castle Rackrent*, probably between 1794 and 1795. The second half was written two years later, as rural unrest intensified, between 1796 and 1798.[21] By 1799 the novel was already in print at Edgeworth's publisher (the radical Joseph Johnson), complete with a preface, postscript, and footnotes to Thady's narrative. But at the last minute Edgeworth added the extensive Glossary, so late that in the first edition it appears at the front. *Castle Rackrent* is, then, a dialogic novel: besides the narrative proper, told by the Irish steward Thady in first person, the novel is introduced and concluded by

[20] Ibid. [21] Butler, *Maria Edgeworth*, 353.

an 'editor', who also 'speaks' in the original notes at the bottom of the page. This editorial presence is strengthened by the last-minute addition of the Glossary, which interrupts Thady's story twenty-one times in what amounts to a competing narrative voice.

What seems most significant in this archaeology of *Castle Rackrent* is that Edgeworth composed the narrative proper, or Thady's tale, without the usual supervision and collaboration with her father. Their literary partnership was already well established, particularly through work on children's stories and educational practice in *The Parent's Assistant* (1796) and *Practical Education* (1798), but Richard Edgeworth's editorial hand could be heavy. As his daughter noted of the drafted pages of her first book, *Letters for Literary Ladies* (1795): 'They are now disfigured by all manner of crooked marks of Papa's critical indignation, besides various abusive margin notes.'[22] Appropriately enough, it is as editor that Richard Edgeworth shows up in *Castle Rackrent*. Some critics argue that he wrote the preface and postscript. What is more certain is that he, along with family friends, recommended the addition of the Glossary, Richard contributing the note on wakes.

This Glossary serves to revise a narrative that Edgeworth described as coming to her whole, without

[22] ME to Sophy Ruxton, Feb. 1794; quoted in F. V. Barry, *Maria Edgeworth: Chosen Letters* (1931; New York, 1979), 48.

a single alteration or correction: 'When, for mere amusement, without any idea of publishing, I began to write a family history as Thady would tell it, he seemed to stand beside me and dictate; and I wrote as fast as my pen could go, the characters all imaginary.'[23] The ease with which Edgeworth adopted this Irish voice suggests a strong empathy with her narrator and his subversive tale. For though Thady apologizes and equivocates, his is the story of an Anglo-Irish landlord's ruin at the hands of Thady's own son. *Castle Rackrent* was on this level an Anglo-Irish nightmare, and perhaps Edgeworth felt all the more free to tell it since she wrote initially with no intention of being widely read. As Ann Weekes suggests, such privacy gave Edgeworth the licence to explore the contradictions and dangers of her colonial context freely,[24] including the ways in which her own marginal status as a woman overlapped with that of a dispossessed Irish Catholic. Going public with such a tale called Richard Edgeworth's progressive bluff; his support for the Glossary and Edgeworth's acquiescence suggest they both felt Thady's voice and the dangerous politics it represented needed to be contained.

The Glossary to *Castle Rackrent* registers strong reservations to Edgeworth's narrative. By adopting an

[23] ME to Mrs Stark, 6 Sept. 1834; quoted in Butler, *Maria Edgeworth*, 240–1.

[24] Ann Owens Weekes, *Irish Women Writers: An Uncharted Tradition* (Lexington, Ky., 1990), 39.

antiquarian tone, the editor approaches Thady's tale as folklore, a regional product to be studied and, in some instances, ridiculed. The very first note, attached to 'Monday morning', evokes the stereotype of the shiftless native Irish, lazy workmen who cannot be trusted. Thus, before Thady 'speaks' a word of his story, his authorial voice is undercut: he is placed firmly within the hierarchical social structure as a labourer who must be policed by gentlemen. This theme of surveillance continues in the Glossary in the note on Irish funeral songs. Regretting that these songs have fallen 'into a sort of slip-shod metre amongst women', the editor maintains that funerals provide one more excuse for the native Irish to shirk their work, and practise 'the habits of profligacy and drunkenness'. He even reports the income lost to landlords from 'time spent in attending funerals' at 'half a million' or even 'double that sum'.

The native Irish as portrayed in the Glossary are in need of governing restraint. Their habits are the more dangerous because infectious: upper-class women are too apt, as one note comments, to embrace the washerwoman and laundry-maid's 'raking pot of tea'. These private female gatherings provide opportunities for 'mutual railleries and mutual confidences' threatening to gentlemen themselves. And presumably gentlemen's wives and daughters are at risk of corruption precisely because they share a colonized status with the native Irish who befriend them.

In these examples the editor of the Glossary represents a patriarchal and metropolitan culture: 'he' intervenes from the margins of Thady's narrative, commenting as a scholarly antiquarian on a regional and subordinate voice. In this way the Glossary attempts to restrain the excesses in Edgeworth's original narrative. But that narrative remained unruly, doubling back on the editor with a subversive irony. For the commencing of his tale on a Monday is just as auspicious as Thady claims. As a colonized man, he seizes the power to narrate a story of liberation: the restoration of Irish land to the native Irish.

The 'Continuation of the Memoirs of the Rackrent Family' is actually the 'History of Sir Conolly Rackrent'. While the first part of *Castle Rackrent* deals with three landlords in thirty pages, the second part spends a full fifty pages on a single Rackrent heir, the last. That Sir Conolly Rackrent is allotted so much space in the narrative reflects his quite different relation to Thady and the Irish Catholic community. Recalling the generous Sir Patrick's close ties with the community, Sir Condy is virtually raised among the Catholic tenants alongside Thady's own son Jason. Indeed, it is Thady who takes over the parental role of transmitting the Rackrent family history to Condy as a boy: 'I told him stories of the family and the blood from which he was sprung, and how he might look forward, if the *then* present man should die without childer, to being at the head of the Castle Rackrent estate' (p. 39). The self-reflexive elements in this passage—of Thady narrating the Rackrent family history within the Rackrent family history—mark a new perspective in the novel: this is Thady's story after all. Indeed, with Thady's education of Condy in the details of inheritance, he symbolically assumes the role of patriarch. From this point on, the narrative becomes as much the tale of the rise of the Quirks as the fall of the Rackrents.

This reversal in the last part of the novel suggests that Edgeworth had, in fact, tried to face up to the implications of her earlier narrative. Although with Sir Condy she seemed to be bringing her story full circle, he does not serve the same function in the novel as the ancestor he is often compared with, Sir Patrick. There was, after all, no real need to make the same point twice; the example of Sir Patrick had already demonstrated well enough the flaws of the dissipative landlord. Rather, with Sir Condy, Edgeworth sought to revive the positive communal aspects associated with Sir Patrick, who 'lived and died a monument of old Irish hospitality'. At the historical moment of rupture in Protestant landlord–Catholic tenant relations, Edgeworth was retesting the old model of the harmonious patriarchal community.

She began by emphasizing, in the early part of the 'Continuation', Condy's social origins in the community he eventually governs as landlord. Part of a remote branch of the Rackrent family, Condy has 'little or no fortune'; we are told that he lives in 'a small but slated house' and attends grammar school with Thady's own son. In a foreshadowing of events to come, Jason even helps him with his lessons. When Condy grows older, he rides with the Rackrent huntsman and comes to know even better the countryside and its people, visiting the poor in their cabins and drinking with them 'a glass of burnt whiskey out of an egg-shell' (p. 39). Edgeworth had herself as a young woman ridden out with her father as he made the rounds on his estate. In fact, it is this early contact with Irish tenants which many critics credit as the source of her realistic portraits of the Irish not only in *Castle Rackrent* but in her three later Irish novels, *Ennui* (1809), *The Absentee* (1812), and *Ormond* (1817). She 'knew' the native Irish as others writing in English did not. And perhaps this new way of knowing them was not just the result of having ridden their fields and visited their homes. She could not, on these occasions, have been knowing Irish tenants as a future landowner. She would, like Thady, have been looking on, from a position of relative privilege but very limited power.

Perhaps this liminal status as a woman writer kept Edgeworth from acquiescing to any nostalgic resolution for her novel, even in a period when symbolically and psychologically such a solution, if only at the level of fiction, must have been tempting. Rather, the positing of a landlord with harmonious communal relations shed light on the very conflict through which she was living. For in portraying Sir Condy as initially in harmony with the community from which he comes, the narrative makes clear that the power relations inherent in hereditary right to land are highly problematic.

The theme is played out in Sir Condy's relations with Thady's son Jason. Condy, seeing that Sir Kit is not likely to have an heir, neglects his legal training and lives on loans from Rackrent tenants, 'promising bargains of leases and lawful interest should he ever come into the estate' (p. 40). Thus, when Condy does inherit the Rackrent estate, he is already in debt. Jason, on the other hand, pursues his legal training, becomes agent to the estate, and systematically acquires the property as Sir Condy is forced to sell land to pay his enormous debts. In this sequence of events, Condy's hereditary right to the land is overturned by Jason's greater personal application and ability. The power of property passes from the paternalistic landlord to the self-made bourgeois professional.

Although critics have argued that as a Catholic Jason could not legally own the Rackrent estate, the opportunity for conversion to Protestantism during this period would have made the transaction possible. The text remains all but silent on the question of religion, but Jason's estrangement from his family suggests that his ambition has led him to value market relations over the ties of a Catholic community. As Thady observes of his son, he 'was grown quite a great gentleman, and had none of his relations near him—no wonder he was no kinder to poor Sir Condy than to his own kith and kin' (p. 62). Presented with the attributes of the stridently self-interested capitalist, Jason's social relations reflect his valorization of the cash nexus. Later in the narrative, when Jason effects the final transfer of property in the Rackrent estate, he is even linked with the expanding markets of capital. Thady describes him as 'sticking to [Sir Condy] as I could not have done at the time if you'd have given both the Indies and Cork to boot' (p. 74). Jason is no hero, even in his own father's narrative.

Thady is caught between the two forms of customary relations that Jason seems to deny—an investment in the hierarchical and reciprocal structure of old feudal ties ('I and mine have lived rent free time out of mind'), and a loyalty to immediate family: 'Well, I did not know what to think—it was hard to be talking ill of my own, and I could not but grieve for my poor master's fine estate, all torn by these vultures of the law; so I said nothing, but just looked on to see how it would all end' (p. 62). Thady's apparent passivity is, of course, countered by his decision 'voluntarily undertaken to publish the Memoirs of the Rackrent Family' (p. 7). In this he mirrors Edgeworth herself, who wrote *Castle Rackrent* while she awaited the outcome of the Protestant–Catholic dispute over the right to the land of Ireland. And, through the very activity of telling the tale, she was formulating new articulations of the conflict. For with Jason she had changed the terms of the existing religious deadlock by introducing the concept of class. He stands as the final illustrative type in *Castle Rackrent*: the bourgeois with increasing access to property and status through capital. What kind of landlord he will make we are not told, though in the narrative the tenants themselves display 'terror at the notion of his coming to be landlord over them' (p. 79). Still, he is manifestly efficient when it comes to keeping estate accounts and there is no particular suggestion in the narrative that he acquires the land unfairly. Rather, like the Edgeworths themselves, Jason secures his title to the estate through legal training and a knowledge of the 'quirks' of the law. As such, he benefits from the same legal system by which the Protestant settlers themselves had established and enforced their legitimacy.

In her second Irish novel, *Ennui*, the son of an Irish peasant forms his character through exertion in legal training and becomes Lord of Glenthron Castle. It was the same prophetic note that Edgeworth had sounded in *Castle Rackrent* with the rise of Jason Quirk. For Edgeworth had seen well enough that the rule of law Protestants brought to Ireland would help produce that group Yeats himself seemed so surprised to see dominating the Irish landscape a century later—the Irish Catholic middle class. Edgeworth's narrative thus implicitly undercuts the cause of the Anglo-Irish in the conflicts of the 1790s, and nowhere more than in

Jason's very naming. For in the Golden Fleece story, it is Jason of a kingdom in Thessaly who is the rightful heir to the throne. A usurping uncle, hoping to be rid of him, sends him on a quest for the golden fleece *by representing it as stolen property*. A rightful heir goes on a quest (for someone else's property) in order to regain his land. The myth manages to evoke the double vision with which Edgeworth must have seen the Protestant–Catholic conflict: as the just claim of the Irish Catholics to the land in Ireland which was possessed by her own Anglo-Irish class.

Castle Rackrent's preface has been called propaganda for the Union of 1800. Although the postscript complicates the views of the preface considerably (ending the novel quite literally on a question mark), the original terms of the Union of 1800 make the charge itself confusing. The English Prime Minister, William Pitt, promised equal political rights to Catholics with the parliamentary union between Great Britain and Ireland, and the Edgeworths believed such a merger would increase investment of English resources in Ireland and improve Irish trade. Moreover, if Maria Edgeworth had given up on a nascent Irish nationalism it may well have been because she understood too well its xenophobic tendencies. The Anglo-Irish had had their chance in 1782 to forge a unified nation when Henry Grattan urged an independent Irish Parliament to include Irish Catholics. Fearing that if they shared political power with Catholics their Irish estates would be reclaimed, the Anglo-Irish delegates refused and the liberatory moment was lost. That the action of *Castle Rackrent* commences before this significant date (which was also the year of Maria Edgeworth's arrival in Ireland at the age of 14) makes the novel a history of men who made such choices: they bungled Irish nationhood as they had bungled their Irish estates.

As things turned out, England did the Irish Catholics decidedly less good than it had promised. George III opposed Pitt's plan for Catholic Emancipation, and Ireland was left with its own Parliament dissolved and most of its population still largely unrepresented in the English Parliament. Though the Edgeworths had no notion this would be the Union's outcome, they had, at the end, opposed it. When the government in Westminster had bribed Irish Parliament members with money, baronies, and peerages, Richard Edgeworth changed his mind and voted against the Union. As Maria Edgeworth put the case: 'England has not any right to do to Ireland *good against her will*.'[25]

Edgeworth's description of Ireland as a woman who is not to be forced, who must give her consent to a union, suggests that the eventual outcome was, if not rape, at least a base seduction. That the metaphor for relations between the two countries became a conjugal one, with England in the role of governing husband,

[25] ME to Sophy Ruxton, 29 Jan. 1800; quoted in Hare, *Life and Letters*, i. 69.

has been documented.[26] But like Jonathan Swift before her, Edgeworth had tried to cast the relationship in *Castle Rackrent* in more sororal terms, describing Ireland in the postscript as a 'sister country' and one which ought to be better known. In this she echoed her contemporary, Charlotte Brooke, who wrote in her preface to *Reliques of Irish Poetry* (1789): 'The British muse is not yet informed that she has an elder sister in this isle; let us then introduce them to each other!'[27] A sister, whether elder or younger, might relate to another sister with relative equality. Maria Edgeworth's first novel contains elements of an Irish nationalism more liberatory perhaps than the Celtic essentialism Yeats later helped to forge. For with the multiple narrative voices of *Castle Rackrent* Edgeworth presents Irish identity as dialogue, sometimes fractious, but always dynamic. And dialogue is central because Irish identity is actively negotiated and constructed, not borne along in the blood.

[26] See C. L. Innes, *Woman and Nation in Irish Literature and Society* (Athens, Ga., 1993).

[27] Charlotte Brooke, *Reliques of Irish Poetry* (1789; Gainsville, Fla., 1970), p. vii.

NOTE ON THE TEXT

THE text is printed from the British Museum copy of the first edition of the novel, published by Joseph Johnson (London, 1800), except that the position of Maria Edgeworth's Glossary, added as an afterthought following the Preface when the novel was already in the press, has been moved to its natural position at the end of the novel—the position it was accorded in the second London edition of 1800, and in all subsequent editions—with its page-references adjusted to the present text. Corrections in the author's hand in the Butler copy of the first edition have been incorporated in the text for the first time and recorded in the notes; and obvious misprints have been corrected.

The publishing history of *Rackrent* after 1800 is not marked by any large changes in the text, in spite of family persuasions, though there is some loss of individuality in punctuation—an individuality which we may fairly attribute to Maria herself, since she wrote the novel, exceptionally, without the advice of her father, and boasted to an aunt of the clearness of her manuscript: 'There was literally not a correction,' she wrote to Mrs Ruxton on 29 January 1800, 'not an alteration, made in the first writing, no copy, and, as I recollect, no interlineation; it went to the press just as it was written.' This argues well for the authority of

1800. The first Dublin edition of *1800* is merely a reprint, with many minor differences in spelling. The third London edition, with some corrections, appeared in 1801, with Maria Edgeworth's name for the first time on the title-page; the fourth in 1804, all octavos; and the duodecimo fifth (with an addition to the Glossary and footnotes deleted) in 1810, all published by Johnson. The fifth was reprinted by Johnson's successor, Hunter, as a sixth edition in 1815. The first collected edition (1825) was carelessly made. The second (1832–3) undoubtedly includes a number of minor corrections made by the novelist or with her approval: spelling is altered and punctuation further simplified, following the trend of the second and later editions, especially by reducing the rather feminine dashes of *1800* and by reducing one of the features of the first edition, the use of brackets within dialogue around phrases like 'says he'. Three footnotes are dropped, and some new misprints introduced. Altogether, *1832* is largely a reprint of the early editions in a more modern, or less idiosyncratic, dress, and for this reason it is clearly of less interest than the epoch-making octavo of January 1800. In an original-spelling edition such as this, it has seemed better to reproduce the conventions of the day in which the novel was written and first read rather than those of a generation and more later. *Rackrent* is a late eighteenth-century novel; and, for the first time, it is reproduced here in its original form.

G.W.

SELECT BIBLIOGRAPHY

BIOGRAPHY

Butler, Harriet Jessie, and Harold Edgeworth Butler (eds.), *The Black Book of Edgeworthstown and Other Edgeworth Memories, 1585–1817* (London: Faber & Gwyer, 1927).

Butler, Marilyn, *Maria Edgeworth: A Literary Biography* (Oxford: Clarendon Press, 1972).

Colvin, Christina, *Maria Edgeworth: Letters from England 1813–1844* (Oxford: Clarendon Press, 1971).

—— *Maria Edgeworth in France and Switzerland* (Oxford: Clarendon Press, 1979).

Edgeworth, Frances, *A Memoir of Maria Edgeworth, with a Selection from Her Letters* (3 vols.; London: Joseph Masters & Son, 1867).

Edgeworth, Richard Lovell, *Memoirs of Richard Lovell Edgeworth: Begun By Himself and Concluded By His Daughter Maria Edgeworth* (2 vols.; Shannon: Irish University Press, 1969).

Hare, Augustus J. C. (ed.), *The Life and Letters of Maria Edgeworth* (2 vols.; London: Edward Arnold, 1894; repr. 1971).

MacDonald, Edgar E. (ed.), *The Education of the Heart: The Correspondence of Rachel Mordecai Lazarus and Maria Edgeworth* (Chapel Hill, NC: The University of North Carolina Press, 1977).

CRITICISM

Butler, Marilyn, *Jane Austen and the War of Ideas* (Oxford: Clarendon Press, 1975).

Cronin, John, *The Anglo-Irish Novel*, i, *The Nineteenth Century* (Belfast: Appletree, 1980).

Deane, Seamus, *A Short History of Irish Literature* (London: Hutchinson, 1986).

Dunne, Tom, *Maria Edgeworth and the Colonial Mind* (Dublin: National University of Ireland, 1985).

Hurst, Michael, *Maria Edgeworth and the Public Scene* (London: Macmillan, 1969).

Kirkpatrick, Kathryn, 'Putting Down the Rebellion: Notes and Glosses on Maria Edgeworth's *Castle Rackrent*', *Éire-Ireland: A Journal of Irish Studies*, 30 (1995).

McCormack, W. J., *Ascendancy and Tradition in Anglo-Irish Literary History from 1789* to *1939* (Oxford: Clarendon Press, 1985).

Mortimer, Anthony, ' "Castle Rackrent" and its Historical Contexts', *Études Irlandaises*, 9 (1984), 107–23.

Newcomer, James, *Maria Edgeworth* (Lewisburg, Pa.: Bucknell University Press, 1973).

Owens, Coilin, *Family Chronicles: Maria Edgeworth's Castle Rackrent* (Dublin: Wolfhound Press, 1987).

Sheeran, P. F., 'Colonists and Colonized: Some Aspects of Anglo-Irish Literature from Swift to Joyce', *Yearbook of English Studies*, 13 (1983), 97–115.

Tracy, Robert, 'Maria Edgeworth and Lady Morgan: Legality versus Legitimacy', *Nineteenth-Century Fiction*, 40/1 (1985), 1–22.

Weekes, Ann Owens, *Irish Women Writers: An Uncharted Tradition* (Lexington, Ky.: The University Press of Kentucky, 1990).

A CHRONOLOGY OF MARIA EDGEWORTH

1767	Jan. Born at Black Bourton, Oxfordshire, second child of Richard Lovell Edgeworth (RLE) (1744–1817)
1773	Death of Maria's mother, Anna Maria Edgeworth (née Elers). RLE marries Honora Sneyd of Lichfield
	Maria's first visit to Ireland
1775–80	At school at Derby
1780	Death of Honora, RLE's second wife
	RLE marries her sister Elizabeth
	Maria at school in Upper Wimpole Street, London
1782	Maria settles in Ireland, at Edgeworthstown, her father's estate in County Longford. Irish Independency established
1787	*The Freeman Family* begun; resumed as *Patronage* in 1809
1791–2	Visit to Clifton
1794	*Castle Rackrent* begun
1795	*Letters for Literary Ladies*, Maria's first book, partly a letter-novel
1796	*The Parent's Assistant*, a collection of children's stories.
1797	Nov. Death of Elizabeth, RLE's third wife
1798	RLE marries Frances Beaufort
	June. *Practical Education*, a textbook for children written with RLE and other members of the family

	Aug. French land in County Mayo
	Sept. Edgeworths take refuge from rebels in Longford; defeat of French
	RLE elected to Irish Parliament
1799	Clifton revisited; RLE and Maria visit Joseph Johnson, her publisher, in a London prison
1800	Jan. *Castle Rackrent*, Maria's first novel, published anonymously with acclaim
1800	Aug. Union of Great Britain and Ireland
1801	*Moral Tales*, a collection of stories for older children
	June. *Belinda*, Maria's first society novel
1802	May. *Essay on Irish Bulls*, a study of popular Irish humour, written with RLE's help
	Oct. Maria and RLE visit Brussels and Paris during Peace of Amiens. In Paris she is wooed by Edelcrantz, a Swedish courtier
1803	March. Return to England on eve of resumption of Napoleonic Wars. Edinburgh
1804	*Popular Tales*, a collection of stories, some written before 1800
1806	*Leonora*, a romantic letter-novel, perhaps written for Edelcrantz
1809	June. *Tales of Fashionable Life*, i–iii, including *Ennui*, an Irish novel written 1803–5
1814	Death of Joseph Johnson; succeeded by Hunter as Maria's publisher until 1827
	Work on *Patronage* resumed
1812	June. *Tales of Fashionable Life*, iv–vi, including *The Absentee*, an Irish novel

1813 April. Visit to London; Maria meets Byron, Humphry Davy

1814 *Patronage*, a long, unpopular novel begun in 1787 and resumed in 1809

Oct. *Waverley* reaches Edgeworthstown; Maria's correspondence with Scott begins

1817 June. Death of Richard Lovell Edgeworth

July. *Harrington* and *Ormond*, two short novels with Preface by the dying RLE, who wrote part of *Ormond*

1820 March. *Memoirs of Richard Lovell Edgeworth, Begun by Himself and Concluded by his Daughter*, an autobiography begun by RLE in 1808–9, finished by Maria in 1819

Maria's second visit to Paris, with her sisters Fanny and Harriet

1823 May. Visit to Scotland; first meeting with Scott in Edinburgh

Aug. Fortnight as Scott's guest at Abbotsford

1825 First collected edition (14 vols.)

1832 Second collected edition (18 monthly vols.), edited by Maria

1833 Visit to Connemara

1834 *Helen*, the last novel, written 1830–3

1849 May. Death of Maria Edgeworth

According to M. Butler and C. Colvin, *Notes & Queries* (September 1971) ME may have been born on 1 January 1768.

CASTLE RACKRENT[1]

AN
HIBERNIAN TALE

TAKEN FROM FACTS,

AND FROM

THE MANNERS OF THE IRISH SQUIRES,

BEFORE THE YEAR 1782[2]

PREFACE[3]

THE prevailing taste of the public for anecdote has been censured and ridiculed by critics, who aspire to the character of superior wisdom: but if we consider it in a proper point of view, this taste is an incontestible proof of the good sense and profoundly philosophic temper of the present times. Of the numbers who study, or at least who read history, how few derive any advantage from their labors! The heroes of history are so decked out by the fine fancy of the professed historian; they talk in such measured prose, and act from such sublime or such diabolical motives, that few have sufficient taste, wickedness or heroism, to sympathize in their fate. Besides, there is much uncertainty even in the best authenticated antient or modern histories; and that love of truth, which in some minds is innate and immutable, necessarily leads to a love of secret memoirs and private anecdotes. We cannot judge either of the feelings or of the characters of men with perfect accuracy from their actions or their appearance in public; it is from their careless conversations, their half finished sentences, that we may hope with the greatest probability of success to discover their real characters. The life of a great or of a little man written by himself, the familiar letters, the diary of any individual published by his friends, or by his enemies after his decease, are esteemed important literary curiosities. We are surely justified in this eager desire to collect the most minute facts relative to the domestic lives, not only of the great and good, but even of the worthless and insignificant, since it is only by a comparison of their actual happiness or misery in the privacy of domestic life, that we can form a just estimate of the real reward of virtue, or the real punishment of vice. That the great are not as happy as they seem, that the external circumstances of fortune and rank do not constitute felicity, is asserted by every moralist; the historian can seldom, consistently with his dignity, pause to illustrate this truth, it is therefore to the biographer we must have recourse. After we have beheld splendid characters playing their parts on the great theatre of the world, with all the advantages of stage effect and decoration, we anxiously beg to be admitted behind the scenes, that we may take a nearer view of the actors and actresses.

Some may perhaps imagine, that the value of biography depends upon the judgment and taste of the biographer; but on the contrary it may be maintained, that the merits of a biographer are inversely as the extent of his intellectual powers and of his literary talents. A plain unvarnished tale[4] is preferable to the most highly ornamented narrative. Where we see that a man has the power, we may naturally suspect that he has the will to deceive us, and those who are used to literary manufacture know how much is often sacrificed to the rounding of a period or the pointing an antithesis.[5]

That the ignorant may have their prejudices as well as the learned cannot be disputed, but we see and despise vulgar errors; we never bow to the authority of him who has no great name to sanction his absurdities. The partiality which blinds a biographer to the defects of his hero, in proportion as it is gross ceases to be dangerous; but if it be concealed by the appearance of candor, which men of great abilities best know how to assume, it endangers our judgment sometimes, and sometimes our morals. If her Grace the Duchess of Newcastle, instead of penning her lord's elaborate eulogium, had undertaken to write the life of Savage,[6] we should not have been in any danger of mistaking an idle, ungrateful libertine, for a man of genius and virtue. The talents of a biographer are often fatal to his reader. For these reasons the public often judiciously countenances those, who without sagacity to discriminate character, without elegance of style to relieve the tediousness of narrative, without enlargement of mind to draw any conclusions from the facts they relate, simply pour forth anecdotes and retail conversations, with all the minute prolixity of a gossip in a country town.

The author of the following memoirs[7] has upon these grounds fair claims to the public favor and attention: he was an illiterate old steward, whose partiality to *the family* in which he was bred and born must be obvious to the reader. He tells the history of the Rackrent family in his vernacular idiom, and in the full confidence that Sir Patrick, Sir Murtagh, Sir Kit,[8] and Sir Condy Rackrent's affairs, will be as interesting to all the world as they were to himself. Those who were acquainted with the manners of a certain class of the gentry of Ireland some years ago, will want no evidence of the truth of honest Thady's narrative: to those who are totally unacquainted with Ireland, the following Memoirs will perhaps be scarcely intelligible, or probably they may appear perfectly incredible. For the information of the *ignorant* English reader a few notes have been subjoined by the editor, and he had it once in contemplation to translate the language of Thady into plain English; but Thady's idiom is incapable of translation, and besides, the authenticity of his story would have been more exposed to doubt if it were not told in his own characteristic manner. Several years ago he related to the editor the history of the Rackrent family, and it was with some difficulty that he was persuaded to have it committed to writing; however, his feelings for '*the honor of the family*,' as he expressed himself, prevailed over his habitual laziness, and he at length completed the narrative which is now laid before the public.

The Editor hopes his readers will observe, that these are 'tales of other times;' that the manners depicted in the following pages are not those of the present age: the race of the Rackrents has long since been extinct in Ireland, and the drunken Sir Patrick, the litigious Sir

Murtagh, the fighting Sir Kit, and the slovenly Sir Condy, are characters which could no more be met with at present in Ireland, than Squire Western or Parson Trulliber[9] in England. There is a time when individuals can bear to be rallied for their past follies and absurdities, after they have acquired new habits and a new consciousness. Nations as well as individuals gradually lose attachment to their identity, and the present generation is amused rather than offended by the ridicule that is thrown upon their ancestors.

Probably we shall soon have it in our power, in a hundred instances, to verify the truth of these observations.

When Ireland loses her identity by an union with Great Britain, she will look back with a smile of good-humoured complacency on the Sir Kits and Sir Condys of her former existence.[10]

AN HIBERNIAN TALE

CASTLE RACKRENT

Monday Morning[g]

HAVING out of friendship for the family, upon whose estate, praised be Heaven! I and mine have lived rent free time out of mind, voluntarily undertaken to publish the Memoirs of the Rackrent Family, I think it my duty to say a few words, in the first place, concerning myself. —My real name is Thady Quirk, though in the family I have always been known by no other than '*honest Thady*'—afterwards, in the time of Sir Murtagh, deceased, I remember to hear them calling me '*old Thady*;' and now I'm come to 'poor Thady'—for I wear a long great coat* winter and summer, which is very handy, as

* The cloak, or mantle, as described by Thady, is of high antiquity.—Spencer,[11] in his 'View of the State of Ireland,' proves that it is not, as some have imagined, peculiarly derived from the Scythians, but that 'most nations of the world antiently used the mantle; for the Jews used it, as you may read of Elias's mantle, &c.; the Chaldees also used it, as you may read in Diodorus; the Egyptians likewise used it, as you may read in Herodotus, and may be gathered by the description of Berenice, in the Greek Commentary upon Callimachus; the Greeks also used it anciently, as appeareth by Venus's mantle lined with stars, though afterwards they changed the form thereof into their cloaks, called Pallia, as some of the Irish also use: and the ancient Latins and Romans used it, as you may read in Virgil, who was a very great

I never put my arms into the sleeves, (they are as good as new,) though, come Holantide next, I've had it these seven years; it holds on by a single button round my neck, cloak fashion—to look at me, you would hardly think 'poor Thady' was the father of attorney Quirk; he is a high gentleman, and never minds what poor Thady says, and having better than 1500 a-year, landed estate, looks down upon honest Thady, but I wash my hands of his doings, and as I have lived so will I die, true and loyal to the family.[14]—The family of the Rackrents is, I am proud to say, one of the most ancient in the kingdom.—Every body knows this is not the old family name, which was O'Shaughlin, related to the Kings of

antiquary, that Evander, when Eneas came to him at his feast, did entertain and feast him, sitting on the ground, and lying on mantles; insomuch as he useth the very word mantile for a mantle,

——— Humi mantilia sternunt.

so that it seemeth that the mantle was a general habit to most nations, and not proper to the Scythians only.'

Spencer knew the convenience of the said mantle, as housing, bedding, and cloathing.

'Iren. Because the commodity doth not countervail the discommodity; for the inconveniences which thereby do arise, are much more many; for it is a fit house for an outlaw, a meet bed for a rebel, and an apt cloak for a thief.—First, the outlaw being, for his many crimes and villainies, banished from the towns and houses of honest men, and wandering in waste places, far from danger of law, maketh his mantle his house, and under it covereth himself from the wrath of Heaven, from the offence of the earth, and from the sight of men. When it raineth, it is his pent-house; when it bloweth, it is his tent; when it freezeth, it is his tabernacle. In summer he can wear it loose; in winter he can wrap it close; at all times he can use it; never heavy, never cumbersome. Likewise for a rebel it is as serviceable; for in this war[12] that he maketh (if at least it deserve the name of war), when he still flieth from his foe, and lurketh in the *thick woods*, (*this should be black bogs*,)[13] and straight passages waiting for advantages; it is his bed, yea, and almost his household-stuff.'

Ireland—but that was before my time.—My grandfather was driver to the great Sir Patrick O'Shaughlin, and I heard him, when I was a boy, telling how the Castle Rackrent estate came to Sir Patrick—Sir Tallyhoo Rackrent was cousin-german to him, and had a fine estate of his own, only never a gate upon it, it being his maxim, that a car was the best gate.—Poor gentleman! he lost a fine hunter and his life, at last, by it, all in one day's hunt.—But I ought to bless that day, for the estate came straight into *the* family, upon one condition, which Sir Patrick O'Shaughlin at the time took sadly to heart, they say, but thought better of it afterwards, seeing how large a stake depended upon it, that he should, by Act of Parliament, take and bear the sirname and arms of Rackrent.

Now it was that the world was to see what was *in* Sir Patrick.—On coming into the estate, he gave the finest entertainment ever was heard of in the country—not a man could stand after supper but Sir Patrick himself, who could sit out the best man in Ireland, let alone the three kingdoms itself.[g]—He had his house, from one year's end to another, as full of company as ever it could hold, and fuller; for rather than be left out of the parties at Castle Rackrent, many gentlemen, and those men of the first consequence and landed estates in the country, such as the O'Neills of Ballynagrotty, and the Moneygawls[15] of Mount Juliet's Town, and O'Shannons of New Town Tullyhog, made it their choice, often and often, when there was no moon to be had for love or money, in long winter nights, to sleep in the chicken house, which Sir Patrick had fitted up for the purpose of accommodating his friends and the public in general, who honoured him with their company unexpectedly at Castle Rackrent; and this went on, I can't tell you how long—the whole country rang with his praises—Long life to him!—I'm sure I love to look upon his picture, now opposite to me; though I never saw him, he must have been a portly gentleman—his neck something short, and remarkable for the largest pimple on his nose, which, by his particular desire, is still extant in his picture—said to be a striking likeness, though taken when young.—He is said also to be the inventor of raspberry whiskey, which is very likely, as nobody has ever appeared to dispute it with him, and as there still exists a broken punch-bowl at Castle-Stopgap, in the garret, with an inscription to that effect—a great curiosity.—A few days before his death he was very merry; it being his honour's birth-day, he called my great grandfather in, God bless him! to drink the company's health, and filled a bumper himself, but could not carry it to his head, on account of the great shake in his hand—on this he cast his joke, saying, 'What would my poor father say to me if he was to pop out of the grave, and see me now?—I remember, when I was a little boy, the first bumper of claret he gave me after dinner, how he praised me for carrying it so steady to my mouth—Here's my thanks to him—a bumper toast'—Then he fell to singing the favourite song he learned from his father—for the last time, poor gentleman—he sung it that night as loud and hearty as ever, with a chorus—

He that goes to bed, and goes to bed sober,
Falls as the leaves do, falls as the leaves do, and dies in October—
But he that goes to bed, and goes to bed mellow,
Lives as he ought to do, lives as he ought to do, and dies an honest fellow.[16]

Sir Patrick died that night—just as the company rose to drink his health with three cheers, he fell down in a sort of a fit, and was carried off—they sat it out, and were surprised, on enquiry, in the morning, to find it was all over with poor Sir Patrick—Never did any gentleman live and die more beloved in the country by rich and poor—his funeral was such a one as was never known before nor since in the county!—All the gentlemen in the three counties were at it—far and near, how they flocked![17]—my great grandfather said, that to see all the women even in their red cloaks, you would have taken them for the army drawn out.—Then such a fine whillaluh![g] you might have heard it to the farthest end of the county, and happy the man who could get but a sight of the hearse!—But who'd have thought it?[18] Just as all was going on right, through his own town they were passing, when the body was seized for debt—a rescue was apprehended from the mob—but the heir who attended the funeral was against that, for fear of consequences, seeing that those villains acted[19] under the disguise of the law—So, to be sure, the law must take its course—and little gain had the creditors for their pains. First and foremost, they had the curses of the country; and Sir Murtagh Rackrent the new heir, in the next place, on account of this affront to the body, refused to pay a shilling of the debts, in which he was countenanced by all the best gentlemen of property, and others of his acquaintance, Sir Murtagh alledging in all companies, that he all along meant to pay his father's debts of honor; but the moment the law was taken of him, there was an end of honor to be sure. It was whispered, (but none but the enemies of the family believe it) that this was all a sham seizure to get quit of the debts, which he had bound himself to pay in honor.

It's a long time ago, there's no saying how it was, but this for certain, the new man did not take at all after the old gentleman—The cellars were never filled after his death—and no open house, or any thing as it used to be—the tenants even were sent away without their whiskey[g]—I was ashamed myself, and knew not what to say for the honor of the family—But I made the best of a bad case, and laid it all at my lady's door, for I did not like *her* any how, nor any body else—she was of the family of the Skinflints, and a widow—It was a strange match for Sir Murtagh; the people in the country thought he demeaned himself greatly[g]—but *I* said nothing—I knew how it was—Sir Murtagh was a great lawyer, and looked to the great Skinflint estate; there, however, he overshot himself; for though one of the co-heiresses, he was never the better for her, for she outlived him many's the long day—he could not foresee that, to be sure, when he married her. I must say for her, she made him the best of wives, being a very notable stirring woman, and looking close to every thing. But I always suspected she had Scotch blood in her veins, any thing else I could have looked over in her from a regard to the family. She was a strict observer for self and servants of Lent, and all Fast days, but not holidays. One of the maids having fainted three times the last day of Lent, to keep soul and body together we put a morsel of roast beef into her mouth, which came from Sir Murtagh's dinner, who never fasted, not he; but somehow or other it unfortunately reached my lady's ears, and the priest of the parish had a complaint made of it the next day, and the poor girl was forced as soon as she could walk to do penance for it, before she could get any peace or absolution in the house or out of it. However, my lady was very charitable in her own way. She had a charity school for poor children, where they were taught to read and write gratis, and where they were kept well to spinning gratis for my lady in return; for she had always heaps of duty yarn from the tenants, and got all her houshold linen out of the estate from first to last; for after the spinning, the weavers on the estate took it in hand for nothing, because of the looms my lady's interest could get from the Linen Board to distribute gratis. Then there was a bleach yard near us, and the tenant dare refuse my lady nothing, for fear of a law-suit Sir Murtagh kept hanging over him about the water course. With these ways of managing, 'tis surprising how cheap my lady got things done, and how proud she was of it. Her table the same way—kept for next to nothing—duty fowls, and duty turkies, and duty geese,[g] came as fast as we could eat 'em, for my lady kept a sharp look out, and knew to a tub of butter every thing the tenants had, all round. They knew her way, and what with fear of driving for rent and Sir Murtagh's law-suits, they were kept in such good order, they never thought of coming near Castle Stopgap without a present of something or other—nothing too much or too little for my lady—eggs—honey—butter—meal—fish—game, growse, and herrings, fresh or salt—all went for something. As for their young pigs, we had them, and the best bacon and hams they could make up, with all young chickens in spring; but they were a set of poor wretches, and we had nothing but misfortunes with them, always breaking and running away—This, Sir Murtagh and my lady said, was all their former landlord Sir Patrick's fault, who let 'em all get the half year's rent into arrear—there was something in that, to be sure—But Sir Murtagh was as much the contrary way—For let alone making English tenants[g] of them, every soul—he was always driving and driving, and pounding and pounding, and canting[g] and canting, and replevying and replevying, and he made a good living of trespassing cattle—there was always some tenant's pig, or horse, or cow, or calf, or goose, trespassing, which was so great a gain to Sir Murtagh, that he did not like to hear me talk of repairing fences. Then his herriots[20] and duty work[g] brought him in something—his turf was cut—his potatoes set and dug—his hay brought home, and in short all the work about his house done for nothing; for in all our leases there were strict clauses with heavy penalties, which Sir Murtagh knew well how to enforce—so many days duty work of man and horse, from every tenant, he was to have, and had, every year; and when a man vexed him, why the finest day he could pitch on, when the cratur was getting in his own harvest, or thatching his cabin, Sir Murtagh made it a principle to call upon him and his horse—so he taught 'em all, as he said, to know the law of landlord and tenant. As for law, I believe no man, dead or alive, ever loved it so well as Sir Murtagh. He had once sixteen suits pending at a time, and I never saw him so much himself — roads — lanes — bogs — wells — ponds — eel-wires — orchards — trees — tythes — vagrants — gravel-pits — sandpits — dung-hills and nuisances—every thing upon the face of the earth furnished him good matter for a suit. He used to boast that he had a law-suit for every letter in the alphabet. How I used to wonder to see Sir Murtagh in the midst of the papers in his office—why he could hardly turn about for them. I made bold to shrug my shoulders once in his presence, and thanked my stars I was not born a gentleman to so much toil and trouble—but Sir Murtagh took me up short with his old proverb, 'learning is better than house or land.'[21] Out of forty-nine suits which he had, he never lost one but seventeen[g];

the rest he gained with costs, double costs, treble costs sometimes—but even that did not pay. He was a very learned man in the law, and had the character of it; but how it was I can't tell, these suits that he carried cost him a power of money—in the end he sold some hundreds a year of the family estate—but he was a very learned man in the law, and I know nothing of the matter except having a great regard for the family. I could not help grieving when he sent me to post up notices of the sale of the fee simple of the lands and appurtenances of Timoleague.—'I know, honest Thady,' says he to comfort me, 'what I'm about better than you do; I'm only selling to get the ready money wanting, to carry on my suit with spirit with the Nugents of Carrickashaughlin.'

He was very sanguine about that suit with the Nugents of Carrickashaughlin. He would have gained it, they say, for certain, had it pleased Heaven to have spared him to us, and it would have been at the least a plump two thousand a year in his way; but things were ordered otherwise, for the best to be sure. He dug up a fairy-mount* against my advice, and had no luck afterwards. Though a learned man in the law, he was a little too incredulous in other matters. I warned him that I heard

* [22] These fairy-mounts [g] are called ant-hills in England. They are held in high reverence by the common people in Ireland. A gentleman, who in laying out his lawn had occasion to level one of these hillocks, could not prevail upon any of his labourers to begin the ominous work. He was obliged to take a *loy*[23] from one of their reluctant hands, and began the attack himself. The labourers agreed, that the vengeance of the fairies would fall upon the head of the presumptuous mortal, who first disturbed them in their retreat.

the very Banshee* that my grandfather heard, before I was born long, under[24] Sir Patrick's window a few days before his death. But Sir Murtagh thought nothing of the Banshee, nor of his cough with a spitting of blood, brought on, I understand, by catching cold in attending the courts, and overstraining his chest with making himself heard in one of his favorite causes. He was a great speaker, with a powerful voice; but his last speech was not in the courts at all. He and my lady, though both of the same way of thinking in some things, and though she was as good a wife and great economist as you could see, and he the best of husbands, as to looking into his affairs, and making money for his family; yet I don't know how it was, they had a great deal of sparring and jarring between them.—My lady had her privy purse—and she had her weed ashes,[g] and her sealing money[g] upon the signing of all the leases, with something to buy gloves besides; and besides again often took money from the tenants, if offered properly, to speak for them to Sir Murtagh about abatements and renewals. Now the weed ashes and the glove money he allowed her clear perquisites; though once when he saw her in a new gown saved out of the weed ashes, he told her to my face, (for he could say a sharp thing) that she should not

* The Banshee is a species of aristocratic fairy, who in the shape of a little hideous old woman has been known to appear, and heard to sing in a mournful supernatural voice under the windows of great houses, to warn the family that some of them are soon to die. In the last century every great family in Ireland had a Banshee, who attended regularly, but latterly their visits and songs have been discontinued.

put on her weeds before her husband's death. But it grew more serious when they came to the renewal businesses. At last, in a dispute about an abatement, my lady would have the last word, and Sir Murtagh grew mad;[g] I was within hearing of the door, and now wish I had made bold to step in. He spoke so loud, the whole kitchen was out on the stairs[g]—All on a sudden he stopped, and my lady too. Something has surely happened, thought I—and so it was, for Sir Murtagh in his passion broke a blood-vessel, and all the law in the land could do nothing in that case. My lady sent for five physicians, but Sir Murtagh died, and was buried. She had a fine jointure settled upon her, and took herself away to the great joy of the tenantry. I never said any thing, one way or the other, whilst she was part of the family, but got up to see her go at three o'clock in the morning—'It's a fine morning, honest Thady, says she; good bye to ye'—and into the carriage she stept, without a word more, good or bad, or even half-a-crown; but I made my bow, and stood to see her safe out of sight for the sake of the family.

Then we were all bustle in the house, which made me keep out of the way, for I walk slow and hate a bustle, but the house was all hurry-skurry, preparing for my new master.—Sir Murtagh, I forgot to notice, had no childer,* so the Rackrent estate went to his younger brother—a young dashing officer—who came amongst

* *Childer*—this is the manner in which many of Thady's rank, and others in Ireland, *formerly* pronounced the word *children*.

us before I knew for the life of me whereabouts I was, in a gig or some of them things, with another spark along with him, and led horses, and servants, and dogs, and scarce a place to put any Christian of them into; for my late lady had sent all the feather-beds off before her, and blankets, and household linen, down to the very knife cloths, on the cars to Dublin, which were all her own, lawfully paid for out of her own money—So the house was quite bare, and my young master, the moment ever he set foot in it out of his gig, thought all those things must come of themselves, I believe, for he never looked after any thing at all, but harum-scarum called for every thing as if we were conjurers, or he in a public-house. For my part, I could not bestir myself any how; I had been so used to my late master and mistress, all was upside down with me, and the new servants in the servants' hall were quite out of my way; I had nobody to talk to, and if it had not been for my pipe and tobacco should, I verily believe, have broke my heart for poor Sir Murtagh.

But one morning my new master caught a glimpse of me as I was looking at his horse's heels, in hopes of a word from him—and is that old Thady! says he, as he got into his gig—I loved him from that day to this, his voice was so like the family—and he threw me a guinea out of his waistcoat pocket, as he drew up the reins with the other hand, his horse rearing too; I thought I never set my eyes on a finer figure of a man—quite another sort from Sir Murtagh, though withal *to* *me*, a family likeness—A fine life we should have led, had he stayed amongst us, God bless him!—he valued a guinea as little as any man—money to him was no more than dirt, and his gentleman and groom, and all belonging to him, the same—but the sporting season over, he grew tired of the place, and having got down a great architect for the house, and an improver for the grounds, and seen their plans and elevations, he fixed a day for settling with the tenants, but went off in a whirlwind to town, just as some of them came into the yard in the morning. A circular letter came next post from the new agent, with news that the master was sailed for England, and he must remit 500l. to Bath for his use, before a fortnight was at an end—Bad news still for the poor tenants, no change still for the better with them—Sir Kit Stopgap, my young master, left all to the agent, and though he had the spirit of a Prince, and lived away to the honour of his country abroad, which I was proud to hear of, what were we the better for that at home? The agent was one of your middle men,* who grind the

* *Middle men.*—There was a class of men termed middle men in Ireland, who took large farms on long leases from gentlemen of landed property, and set the land again in small portions to the poor, as under tenants, at exorbitant rents. The *head-landlord*, as he *was* called, seldom saw his *under tenants*, but if he could not get the *middle man* to pay him his rent punctually, he *went to the land, and drove the land for his rent*, that is to say, he sent his steward or bailiff, or driver, to the land, to seize the cattle, hay, corn, flax, oats, or potatoes, belonging to the under-tenants, and proceeded to sell these for his rent; it sometimes happened that these unfortunate tenants paid their rent twice over, once to the *middle man*, and once to the *head landlord*.

The characteristics of a middle man *were*, servility to his superiors, and tyranny[25] towards his inferiors—The poor detested this race of beings. In face of the poor, and can never bear a man with a hat upon his head—he ferretted the tenants out of their lives—not a week without a call for money—drafts upon drafts from Sir Kit—but I laid it all to the fault of the agent; for, says I, what can Sir Kit do with so much cash, and he a single man? but still it went.—Rents must be all paid up to the day, and afore—no allowance for improving tenants—no consideration for those who had built upon their farms—No sooner was a lease out, but the land was advertised to the highest bidder—all the old tenants turned out, when they had spent their substance in the hope and trust of a renewal from the landlord.—All was now set at the highest penny to a parcel of poor wretches who meant to run away, and did so, after taking two crops out of the ground. Then fining down the year's rent[g] came into fashion—any thing for the ready penny, and with all this, and presents to the agent and the driver,[g] there was no such thing as standing it—I said nothing, for I had a regard for the family, but I walked about, thinking if his honour Sir Kit, (long may he live to reign over us!) knew all this, it would go hard with him, but he'd see us righted—not that I had any thing for my own share to complain of, for the agent was always very civil to me, when he came down into the

speaking to them, however, they always used the most abject language, and the most humble tone and posture—'*Please your honour,—and please your honour's honour*,' they knew must be repeated as a charm at the beginning and end of every equivocating, exculpatory, or supplicatory sentence—and they were much more alert in doffing their caps to these new men, than to those of what they call *good old families*.—A witty carpenter once termed these middle men *journeymen-gentlemen*.

country, and took a great deal of notice of my son Jason. —Jason Quirk, though he be my son, I must say, was a good scholar from his birth, and a very 'cute lad—I thought to make him a priest,[g] but he did better for himself—Seeing how he was as good a clerk as any in the county, the agent gave him his rent accounts to copy, which he did first of all for the pleasure of obliging the gentleman, and would take nothing at all for his trouble, but was always proud to serve the family.—By and by, a good farm bounding us to the east fell into his honour's hands, and my son put in a proposal for it; why shouldn't he as well as another?—The proposals all went over to the master at the Bath, who knowing no more of the land than the child unborn, only having once been out a grousing on it before he went to England; and the value of lands, as the agent informed him, falling every year in Ireland, his honour wrote over in all haste a bit of a letter, saying he left it all to the agent, and that he must set it as well as he could to the best bidder, to be sure, and send him over £200. by return of post: with this the agent gave me a hint, and I spoke a good word for my son, and gave out in the country, that nobody need bid against us.—So his proposal was just the thing, and he a good tenant; and he got a promise of an abatement in the rent, after the first year, for advancing the half year's rent at signing the lease, which was wanting to compleat the agent's £200, by the return of the post, with all which my master wrote back he was well satisfied.— About this time we learned from the agent, as a great secret, how the money went so fast, and the reason of the thick coming of the master's drafts: he was a little too fond of play, and Bath, they say, was no place for a young man of his fortune, where there were so many of his own countrymen too haunting him up and down, day and night, who had nothing to lose—at last, at Christmas, the agent wrote over to stop the drafts, for he could raise no more money on bond or mortgage, or from the tenants, or any how, nor had he any more to lend himself, and desired at same time to decline the agency for the future, wishing Sir Kit his health and happiness, and the compliments of the season—for I saw the letter before ever it was sealed, when my son copied it.—When the answer came, there was a new turn in affairs, and the agent was turned out; and my son Jason, who had corresponded privately with his honor occasionally on business, was forthwith desired by his honor to take the accounts into his own hands, and look them over till further orders—It was a very spirited letter, to be sure: Sir Kit sent his service, and the compliments of the season, in return to the agent, and he would fight him with pleasure to-morrow, or any day, for sending him such a letter, if he was born a gentleman, which he was sorry (for both their sakes) to find (too late) he was not.—Then, in a private postscript, he condescended to tell us that all would be speedily settled to his satisfaction, and we should turn over a new leaf, for he was going to be married in a fortnight to the grandest heiress in England, and had only immediate occasion at present for £200, as he would not choose to touch his lady's fortune for travelling expences home to Castle Rackrent, where he intended to be, wind and weather permitting, early in the next month, and desired fires, and the house to be painted, and the new building to go on as fast as possible, for the reception of him and his lady before that time—with several words besides in the letter, which we could not make out, because, God bless him! he wrote in such a flurry—My heart warmed to my new lady when I read this; I was almost afraid it was too good news to be true—but the girls fell to scouring, and it was well they did, for we soon saw his marriage in the paper to a lady with I don't know how many tens of thousand pounds to her fortune—then I watched the post-office for his landing, and the news came to my son of his and the bride being in Dublin, and on the way home to Rackrent Gap—We had bonfires all over the country, expecting him down the next day, and we had his coming of age still to celebrate, which he had not time to do properly before he left the country; therefore a great ball was expected, and great doings upon his coming, as it were, fresh to take possession of his ancestors' estate.—I never shall forget the day he came home—we had waited and waited all day long till eleven o'clock at night, and I was thinking of sending the boy to lock the gates, and giving them up for that night, when there come the carriages thundering up to the great hall door—I got the first sight of the bride; for when the carriage door opened, just as she had her foot on the steps, I held the flam[g] full in her face to light her, at which she shuts her eyes, but I had a full view of the rest of her, and greatly shocked I was, for by that light she was little better than a blackamoor, and seemed crippled, but that was only sitting so long in the chariot—'You're kindly welcome to Castle Rackrent, my lady,' says I, (recollecting who she was)—'Did your honor hear of the bonfires?' His honor spoke never a word, nor so much as handed her up the steps;[26] he looked to me no more like himself than nothing at all; I know I took him for the skeleton of his honor—I was not sure what to say next to one or t'other, but seeing she was a stranger in a foreign country, I thought it but right to speak chearful to her, so I went back again to the bonfires—'My lady (says I, as she crossed the hall) there would have been fifty times as many, but for fear of the horses and frightening your ladyship—Jason and I forbid them, please your honor.' —With that she looked at me a little bewildered—'Will I have a fire lighted in the state room to-night?' was the next question I put to her—but never a word she answered, so I concluded she could not speak a word of English, and was from foreign parts—The short and the long of it was, I couldn't tell what to make of her, so I left her to herself, and went straight down to the servants' hall to learn something for certain about her. Sir Kit's own man was tired, but the groom set him a talking at last, and we had it all out before ever I closed my eyes that night. The bride might well be a great fortune—she was a *Jewish* by all accounts, who are famous for their great riches. I had never seen any of that tribe or nation before, and could only gather that she spoke a strange kind of English of her own, that she could not abide pork or sausages, and went neither to church nor mass.—Mercy upon his honor's poor soul, thought I, what will become of him and his, and all of us, with this heretic Blackamore[27] at the head of the Castle Rackrent estate. I never slept a wink all night for thinking of it, but before the servants I put my pipe in my mouth and kept my mind to myself; for I had a great regard for the family, and after this when strange gentlemen's servants came to the house, and would begin to talk about the bride, I took care to put the best foot foremost, and passed her for a Nabob, in the kitchen, which accounted for her dark complexion, and every thing.

The very morning after they came home, however, I saw how things were, plain enough, between Sir Kit and my lady, though they were walking together arm in arm after breakfast, looking at the new buildings and the improvements. 'Old Thady, (said my master, just as he used to do) how do you do?'—'Very well, I thank your honor's honor,' said I, but I saw he was not well pleased, and my heart was in my mouth as I walked along after him—'Is the large room damp, Thady?' said his honor—'Oh, damp, your honor! how should it but be as dry as a bone, (says I) after all the fires we have kept in it day and night—It's the barrack room[g] your honor's talking on'—'And what is a barrack room, pray, my dear'—were the first words I ever heard out of my lady's lips—'No matter, my dear,' said he, and went on talking to me, ashamed like I should witness her ignorance.—To be sure to hear her talk, one might have taken her for an innocent,[g] for it was 'what's this, Sir Kit? and what's that, Sir Kit?' all the way we went—To be sure, Sir Kit had enough to do to answer her—'And what do you call that, Sir Kit? (said she) that, that looks like a pile of black bricks, pray Sir Kit?' 'My turf stack, my dear,' said my master, and bit his lip—Where have you lived, my lady, all your life, not to know a turf stack when you see it, thought I, but I said nothing. Then, by-and-by, she takes out her glass and begins spying over the country—'And what's all that black swamp out yonder, Sir Kit?' says she—'My bog, my dear,' says he, and went on whistling—'It's a very ugly prospect, my dear,' says she—'You don't see it, my dear, (says he) for we've planted it out, when the trees grow up, in summer time,' says he—'Where are the trees, (said she) my dear,' still looking through her glass—'You are blind, my dear, (says he) what are these under your eyes?'—'These shrubs?' said she—'Trees,' said he—'May be they are what you call trees in Ireland, my dear, (says she) but they are not a yard high, are they?'—'They were planted out but last year, my lady' says I, to soften matters between them, for I saw she was going the way to make his honor mad with her—'they are very well grown for their age, and you'll not see the bog of Allyballycarricko'shaughlin at all at all through the skreen, when once the leaves come out—But, my lady, you must not quarrel with any part or parcel of Allyballycarricko'shaughlin, for you don't know how many hundred years that same bit of bog has been in the family, we would not part with the bog of Allyballycarricko'shaughlin upon no account at all; it cost the late Sir Murtagh two hundred good pounds to defend his title to it, and boundaries, against the O'Learys, who cut a road through it.'—Now one would have thought this would have been hint enough for my lady, but she fell to laughing like one out of their right mind, and made me say the name of the bog over for her to get it by heart a dozen times—then she must ask me how to spell it, and what was the meaning of it in English—Sir Kit standing by whistling all the while—I verily believe she laid the corner stone of all her future misfortunes at that very instant—but I said no more, only looked at Sir Kit.

There were no balls, no dinners, no doings, the country was all disappointed—Sir Kit's gentleman said, in a whisper to me, it was all my lady's own fault, because she was so obstinate about the cross—'What cross? (says I) is it about her being a heretic?'—'Oh, no such matter, (says he) my master does not mind her heresies, but her diamond cross, it's worth I can't tell you how much, and she has thousands of English pounds concealed in diamonds about her, which she as good as promised to give up to my master before he married, but now she won't part with any of them, and she must take the consequences.'

Her honey-moon, at least her Irish honey-moon, was scarcely well over, when his honour one morning said to me—'Thady, buy me a pig!'—and then the sausages were ordered, and here was the first open breaking out of my lady's troubles—my lady came down herself into the kitchen to speak to the cook about the sausages, and desired never to see them more at her table.—Now my master had ordered them, and my lady knew that—the cook took my lady's part, because she never came down into the kitchen, and was young and innocent in house-keeping, which raised her pity; besides, said she, at her own table, surely, my lady should order and disorder what she pleases—but the cook soon changed her note, for my master made it a principle to have the sausages, and swore at her for a Jew herself, till he drove her fairly out of the kitchen—then for fear of her place, and because he threatened that my lady should give her no discharge without the sausages, she gave up, and from that day forward always sausages or bacon, or pig meat, in some shape or other, went up to table; upon which my lady shut herself up in her own room, and my master said she might stay there, with an oath; and to make sure of her, he turned the key in the door, and kept it ever after in his pocket—We none of us ever saw or heard her speak for seven years after that*—he carried her dinner

* This part of the history of the Rackrent family can scarcely be thought credible; but in justice to honest Thady, it is hoped the reader will recollect the history of the celebrated Lady Cathcart's conjugal imprisonment.[28]—The Editor was acquainted with Colonel M'Guire, Lady Cathcart's husband; he has lately seen and questioned the maid-servant who lived with Colonel

himself—then his honour had a great deal of company to dine with him, and balls in the house, and was as gay and gallant, and as much himself as before he was married—and at dinner he always drank my lady Rackrent's good health, and so did the company, and he sent out always a servant, with his compliments to my Lady Rackrent, and the company was drinking her

M'Guire during the time of Lady Cathcart's imprisonment.—Her Ladyship was locked up in her own house for many years; during which period her husband was visited by the neighbouring gentry, and it was his regular custom at dinner to send his compliments to Lady Cathcart, informing her that the company had the honor to drink her ladyship's health, and begging to know whether there was any thing at table that she would like to eat? the answer was always—'Lady Cathcart's compliments, and she has every thing she wants'—An instance of honesty in a poor Irishwoman deserves to be recorded.—Lady Cathcart had some remarkably fine diamonds, which she had concealed from her husband, and which she was anxious to get out of the house, lest he should discover them: she had neither servant nor friend to whom she could entrust them; but she had observed a poor beggar-woman who used to come to the house—she spoke to her from the window of the room in which she was confined—the woman promised to do what she desired, and Lady Cathcart threw a parcel, containing the jewels, to her.—The poor woman carried them to the person to whom they were directed; and several years afterwards, when Lady Cathcart recovered her liberty, she received her diamonds safely.

At Colonel M'Guire's death, her ladyship was released.—The Editor, within this year, saw the gentleman who accompanied her to England after her husband's death.—When she first was told of his death, she imagined that the news was not true, and that it was told only with an intention of deceiving her.—At his death she had scarcely cloaths sufficient to cover her; she wore a red wig, looked scared, and her understanding seemed stupified; she said that she scarcely knew one human creature from another: her imprisonment lasted above twenty years.—These circumstances may appear strange to an English reader; but there is no danger in the present times, that any individual should exercise such tyranny as Colonel M'Guire's with impunity, the power being now all in the hands of government, and there being no possibility of obtaining from Parliament an act of indemnity for any cruelties.

ladyship's health, and begged to know if there was any thing at table he might send her; and the man came back, after the sham errand, with my lady Rackrent's compliments, and she was very much obliged to Sir Kit—she did not wish for any thing, but drank the company's health.—The country, to be sure, talked and wondered at my lady's being shut up, but nobody chose to interfere or ask any impertinent questions, for they knew my master was a man very apt to give a short answer himself, and likely to call a man out for it afterwards—he was a famous shot—had killed his man before he came of age, and nobody scarce dare look at him whilst at Bath.—Sir Kit's character was so well known in the county, that he lived in peace and quietness ever after, and was a great favorite with the ladies, especially when in process of time, in the fifth year of her confinement, my lady Stopgap fell ill, and took entirely to her bed, and he gave out that she was now skin and bone, and could not last through the winter.—In this he had two physicians' opinions to back him (for now he called in two physicians for her), and tried all his arts to get the diamond cross from her on her death bed, and to get her to make a will in his favour of her separate possessions—but she was there too tough for him—He used to swear at her behind her back, after kneeling to her to her face, and call her, in the presence of his gentleman, his stiff-necked Israelite, though before he married her, that same gentleman told me he used to call her (how he could bring it out I don't know!) 'my pretty Jessica'[29]—To be sure, it must have been hard for her to guess what sort of a husband he reckoned to make her—when she was lying, to all expectation, on her death-bed, of a broken heart, I could not but pity her, though she was a Jewish; and considering too it was no fault of her's to be taken with my master so young as she was at the Bath, and so fine a gentleman as Sir Kit was when he courted her—and considering too, after all they had heard and seen of him as a husband, there were now no less than three ladies in our county talked of for his second wife, all at daggers drawing with each other, as his gentleman swore, at the balls, for Sir Kit for their partner—I could not but think them bewitched, but they all reasoned with themselves, that Sir Kit would make a good husband to any Christian, but a Jewish, I suppose, and especially as he was now a reformed rake; and it was not known how my lady's fortune was settled in her will, nor how the Castle Rackrent estate was all mortgaged, and bonds out against him, for he was never cured of his gaming tricks—but that was the only fault he had, God bless him!

My lady had a sort of fit, and it was given out she was dead, by mistake; this brought things to a sad crisis for my poor master—one of the three ladies shewed his letters to her brother, and claimed his promises, whilst another did the same. I don't mention names—Sir Kit, in his defence, said he would meet any man who dared question his conduct, and as to the ladies, they must settle it amongst them who was to be his second, and his third, and his fourth, whilst his first was still alive, to his mortification and theirs. Upon this, as upon all former occasions, he had the voice of the country with him, on account of the great spirit and propriety he acted with.—He met and shot the first lady's brother—the next day he called out the second, who had a wooden leg, and their place of meeting by appointment being in a new ploughed field, the wooden leg man stuck fast in it.—Sir Kit seeing his situation, with great candour fired his pistol over his head, upon which the seconds interposed, and convinced the parties there had been a slight misunderstanding between them; thereupon they shook hands cordially, and went home to dinner together.—This gentleman, to shew the world how they stood together, and by the advice of the friends of both parties to re-establish his sister's injured reputation, went out with Sir Kit as his second, and carried his message next day to the last of his adversaries.—I never saw him in such fine spirits as that day he went out—sure enough he was within aims-ace[30] of getting quit handsomely of all his enemies; but unluckily, after hitting the toothpick out of his adversary's finger and thumb, he received a ball in a vital part, and was brought home, in little better than an hour after the affair, speechless, on a hand-barrow, to my lady; we got the key out of his pocket the first thing we did, and my son Jason ran to unlock the barrack-room, where my lady had been shut up for seven years, to acquaint her with the fatal accident.—The surprize bereaved her of her senses at first, nor would she believe but we were putting some new trick upon her, to entrap her out of her jewels, for a great while, till Jason bethought himself of taking her to the window, and shewed her the men bringing Sir Kit up the avenue upon the hand-barrow, which had immediately the desired effect; for directly she burst into tears, and pulling her cross from her bosom, she kissed it with as great devotion as ever I witnessed, and lifting up her eyes to Heaven, uttered some ejaculation, which none present heard—but I take the sense of it to be, she returned thanks for this unexpected interposition in her favour, when she had least reason to expect it.—My master was greatly lamented—there was no life in him when we lifted him off the barrow, so he was laid out immediately, and *waked* the same night.—The country was all in an uproar about him, and not a soul but cried shame upon his murderer, who would have been hanged surely, if he could have been brought to his trial whilst the gentlemen in the county were up about it, but he very prudently withdrew himself to the continent before the affair was made public.—As for the young lady who was the immediate cause of the fatal accident, however innocently, she could never shew her head after at the balls in the county or any place, and by the advice of her friends and physicians she was ordered soon after to Bath, where it was expected, if any where on this side of the grave, she would meet with the recovery of her health and lost peace of mind.—As a proof of his great popularity, I need only add, that there was a song made upon my master's untimely death in the newspapers, which was in every body's mouth, singing up and down through the country, even down to the mountains, only three days after his unhappy exit.—He was also greatly bemoaned at the Curragh,[g] where his cattle were well known, and all who had taken up his bets formerly were particularly inconsolable for his loss to society.—His stud sold at the cant[g] at the greatest price ever known in the country; his favourite horses were chiefly disposed of amongst his particular friends, who would give any price for them for his sake; but no ready money was required by the new heir, who wished not to displease any of the gentlemen of the neighbourhood just upon his coming to settle amongst them; so a long credit was given where requisite, and the cash has never been gathered in from that day to this.

But to return to my lady.—She got surprisingly well after my master's decease. No sooner was it known for certain that he was dead, than all the gentlemen within twenty miles of us came in a body as it were, to set my lady at liberty, and to protest against her confinement, which they now for the first time understood was against her own consent. The ladies too were as attentive as possible, striving who should be foremost with their morning visits; and they that saw the diamonds spoke very handsomely of them, but thought it a pity they were not bestowed, if it had so pleased God, upon a lady who would have become them better. All these civilities wrought little with my lady, for she had taken an unaccountable prejudice against the country and every thing belonging to it, and was so partial to her native land, that after parting with the cook, which she did immediately upon my master's decease, I never knew her easy one instant, night or day, but when she was packing up to leave us. Had she meant to make any stay in Ireland, I stood a great chance of being a great favorite with her, for when she found I understood the weather-cock, she was always finding some pretence to be talking to me, and asking me which way the wind blew, and was it likely, did I think, to continue fair for England.—But when I saw she had made up her mind to spend the rest of her days upon her own income and jewels in England, I considered her quite as a foreigner, and not at all any longer as part of the family.—She gave no vails[31] to the servants at Castle Rackrent at parting, notwithstanding the old proverb of '*as rich as a Jew*,' which, she being a Jewish, they built upon with reason—But from first to last she brought nothing but misfortunes amongst us; and if it had not been all along with her, his honor Sir Kit would have been now alive in all appearance.—Her diamond cross was, they say, at the bottom of it all; and it was a shame for her, being his wife, not to show more duty, and to have given it up when he condescended to ask so often for such a bit of a trifle in his distresses, especially when he all along made it no secret he married for money.—But we will not bestow another thought upon her—This much I thought it lay upon my conscience to say, in justice to my poor master's memory.

'Tis an ill wind that blows nobody no good—the same wind that took the Jew Lady Rackrent over to England brought over the new heir to Castle Rackrent.

Here let me pause for breath in my story, for though I had a great regard for every member of the family, yet without compare Sir Conolly, commonly called for short amongst his friends Sir Condy Rackrent, was ever my great favorite, and indeed the most universally beloved man I had ever seen or heard of, not excepting his great ancestor Sir Patrick, to whose memory he, amongst other instances of generosity, erected a handsome marble stone in the church of Castle Rackrent, setting forth in large letters his age, birth, parentage, and many other virtues, concluding with the compliment so justly due, that 'Sir Patrick Rackrent lived and died a monument of old Irish hospitality.'

CONTINUATION[32] OF THE MEMOIRS OF THE RACKRENT FAMILY

HISTORY OF SIR CONOLLY RACKRENT

SIR Condy Rackrent, by the grace of God heir at law to the Castle Rackrent estate, was a remote branch of the family: born to little or no fortune of his own, he was bred to the bar, at which having many friends to push him, and no mean natural abilities of his own, he doubtless would in process of time, if he could have borne the drudgery of that study, have been rapidly made king's counsel at the least—But things were disposed of otherwise, and he never went circuit but twice, and then made no figure for want of a fee, and being unable to speak in public. He received his education chiefly in the college of Dublin; but before he came to years of discretion, lived in the country in a small but slated house, within view of the end of the avenue. I remember him barefooted and headed, running through the street of O'Shaughlin's town, and playing at pitch and toss, ball, marbles, and what not, with the boys of the town, amongst whom my son Jason was a great favorite with him. As for me, he was ever my white-headed boy*—often's the time when I would call in at his father's, where I was always made welcome, he would slip down to me in the kitchen, and love to sit on my knee whilst I told him stories of the family and the blood from which he was sprung, and how he might look forward, if the *then* present man should die without childer, to being at the head of the Castle Rackrent estate.—This was then spoke quite and clear at random to please the child, but it pleased Heaven to accomplish my prophecy afterwards, which gave him a great opinion of my judgment in business. He went to a little grammar school with many others, and my son amongst the rest, who was in his class, and not a little useful to him in his book learning, which he acknowledged with gratitude ever after. These rudiments of his education thus completed, he got a horseback, to which exercise he was ever addicted, and used to gallop over the country whilst yet but a slip of a boy, under the care of Sir Kit's huntsman, who was very fond of him, and often lent him his gun and took him out a shooting under his own eye. By these means he became well acquainted and popular amongst the poor in the neighbourhood early, for there was not a cabin at which he had not stopped some morning or other along with the huntsman, to drink a glass of burnt whiskey out of an egg-shell, to do him good, and warm

* *White-headed boy*—is used by the Irish as an expression of fondness.—It is upon a par with the English term *crony*.—We are at a loss for the derivation of this term.[33]

his heart, and drive the cold out of his stomach.—The old people always told him he was a great likeness of Sir Patrick, which made him first have an ambition to take after him, as far as his fortune should allow. He left us when of an age to enter the college, and there completed his education and nineteenth year; for as he was not born to an estate, his friends thought it incumbent on them to give him the best education which could be had for love or money, and a great deal of money consequently was spent upon him at college and Temple—He was very little altered for the worse, by what he saw there of the great world, for when he came down into the country to pay us a visit we thought him just the same man as ever, hand and glove with every one, and as far from high, though not without his own proper share of family pride, as any man ever you see. Latterly, seeing how Sir Kit and the *Jewish* lived together, and that there was no one between him and the Castle Rackrent estate, he neglected to apply to the law as much as was expected of him, and secretly many of the tenants, and others, advanced him cash upon his note of hand value received, promising bargains of leases and lawful interest should he ever come into the estate.—All this was kept a great secret, for fear the present man hearing of it should take it into his head to take it ill of poor Condy, and so should cut him off for ever by levying a fine, and suffering a recovery to dock the entail[g]—Sir Murtagh would have been the man for that, but Sir Kit was too much taken up philandering to consider the law in this case—or any other.—These practices I have mentioned account for the state of his affairs, I mean Sir Condy's, upon his coming into the Castle Rackrent estate.—He could not command a penny of his first year's income, which, and keeping no accounts, and the great sight of company he did, with many other causes too numerous to mention, was the origin of his distresses.—My son Jason, who was now established agent, and knew every thing, explained matters out of the face to Sir Conolly, and made him sensible of his embarrassed situation. With a great nominal rent-roll, it was almost all paid away in interest, which being for convenience suffered to run on, soon doubled the principal, and Sir Condy was obligated to pass new bonds for the interest, now grown principal, and so on. Whilst this was going on, my son requiring to be paid for his trouble, and many years service in the family gratis, and Sir Condy not willing to take his affairs into his own hands, or to look them even in the face, he gave my son a bargain of some acres which fell out of lease at a reasonable rent; Jason set the land as soon as his lease was sealed to under-tenants, to make the rent, and got two hundred a year profit rent, which was little enough, considering his long agency.—He bought the land at twelve years purchase two years afterwards, when Sir Condy was pushed for money on an execution, and was at the same time allowed for his improvements thereon. There was a sort of hunting lodge upon the estate convenient to my son Jason's land, which he had his eye upon about this time; and he was a little jealous of Sir Condy, who talked of setting it to a stranger, who was just come into the country—Captain Moneygawl was the man; he was son and heir to the Moneygawls of Mount Juliet's town, who had a great estate in the next county to ours, and my master was loth to disoblige the young gentleman, whose heart was set upon the lodge; so he wrote him back that the lodge was at his service, and if he would honor him with his company at Castle Rackrent, they could ride over together some morning and look at it before signing the lease.—Accordingly the Captain came over to us, and he and Sir Condy grew the greatest friends ever you see, and were for ever out a shooting or a hunting together, and were very merry in the evenings, and Sir Condy was invited of course to Mount Juliet's town, and the family intimacy that had been in Sir Patrick's time was now recollected, and nothing would serve Sir Condy but he must be three times a week at the least with his new friends—which grieved me, who knew by the Captain's groom and gentleman how they talked of him at Mount Juliet's town, making him quite, as one may say, a laughing stock and a butt for the whole company: but they were soon cured of *that* by an accident that surprised 'em not a little, as it did me.—There was a bit of a scrawl found upon the waiting maid of old Mr. Moneygawl's youngest daughter Miss Isabella, that laid open the whole; and her father, they say, was like one out of his right mind, and swore it was the last thing he ever should have thought of when he invited my master to his house, that his daughter should think of such a match.—But their talk signified not a straw; for as Miss Isabella's maid reported, her young mistress was fallen over head and ears in love with Sir Condy, from the first time that ever her brother brought him into the house to dinner: the servant who waited that day bchind my master's chair was the first who knew it, as he says; though it's hard to believe him, for he did not tell till a great while afterwards; but however, it's likely enough as the thing turned out that he was not far out of the way; for towards the middle of dinner, as he says, they were talking of stage plays, having a play-house, and being great play actors at Mount Juliet's town, and Miss Isabella turns short to my master and says—'Have you seen the play-bill, Sir Condy?'—'No, I have not,' said he.—'Then more shame for you, (said the Captain her brother) not to know that my sister is to play Juliet to-night, who plays it better than any woman on or off the stage in all Ireland.'—'I am very happy to hear it,' said Sir Condy, and there the matter dropped for the present; but Sir Condy all this time, and a great while afterwards, was at a terrible nonplus, for he had no liking not he to stage plays, nor to Miss Isabella either; to his mind, as it came out over a bowl of whiskey punch at home, his little Judy M'Quirk, who was daughter to a sister's son of mine, was worth twenty of Miss Isabella —He had seen her often when he stopped at her father's cabin to drink whiskey out of the egg-shell, out of hunting, before he came to the estate, and as she gave out was under something like a promise of marriage to her—Any how I could not but pity my poor master, who was so bothered between them, and he an easy-hearted man that could not disoblige nobody, God bless him. To be sure it was not his place to behave ungenerous to Miss Isabella, who had disobliged all her relations for his sake, as he remarked; and then she was locked up in her chamber and forbid to think of him any more, which raised his spirit, because his family was, as he observed, as good as theirs at any rate, and the Rackrents a suitable match for the Moneygawls any day in the year; all which was true enough; but it grieved me to see that upon the strength of all this Sir Condy was growing more in the mind to carry off Miss Isabella to Scotland, in spite of her relations, as she desired.

'It's all over with our poor Judy!' said I, with a heavy sigh, making bold to speak to him one night when he was a little cheerful, and standing in the servant's hall all alone with me, as was often his custom—'Not at all (said he) I never was fonder of Judy than at this present speaking, and to prove it to you, (said he, and he took from my hand a halfpenny, change that I had just got along with my tobacco); and to prove it to you, Thady, says he, it's a toss up with me which I shall marry this minute, her or Mr. Moneygawl of Mount Juliet's Town's daughter—so it is'—'Oh, boo! boo*! (says I, making light of it, to see what he would go on to next)—your honor's joking, to be sure, there's no compare between our poor

* *Boo! Boo!* an exclamation equivalent to *Pshaw!* or *Nonsense.*

Judy and Miss Isabella, who has a great fortune, they say.'—'I'm not a man to mind a fortune, nor never was, (said Sir Condy proudly,) whatever her friends may say; and to make short of it, (says he) I'm come to a determination upon the spot;' with that he swore such a terrible oath, as made me cross myself*—'and by this book, (said he, snatching up my ballad book, mistaking it for my prayer-book, which lay in the window)—and by this book, (said he) and by all the books that ever were shut and opened—it's come to a toss up with me, and I'll stand or fall by the toss, and so, Thady, hand me over that *pin*† out of the ink-horn,' and he makes a cross on the smooth side of the halfpenny[34]—'Judy M'Quirk, (said he) her mark,‡' God bless him! his hand was a little unsteadied by all the whiskey punch he had taken, but it was plain to see his heart was for poor Judy.—My heart was all as one as in my mouth, when I saw the halfpenny up in the air, but I said nothing at all, and when it came down, I was glad I had kept myself to myself, for to be sure now it was all over with poor

* *As made me cross myself*—The Roman Catholics.[35]

† *Pin* read *pen*—it formerly was vulgarly pronounced *pin* in Ireland.

‡ *Her mark*—It *was* the custom in Ireland for those who could not write, to make a cross to stand for their signature, as was formerly the practice of our English monarchs.—The Editor inserts the facsimile of an Irish *mark*, which may hereafter be valuable to a judicious antiquary—

Her
Judy × M'Quirk
Mark.

In bonds or notes, signed in this manner, a witness is requisite, as the name is frequently written by him or her.

Judy.—'Judy's out a luck,' said I, striving to laugh—'I'm out a luck,' said he, and I never saw a man look so cast down; he took up the halfpenny off the flag, and walked away quite sobered like by the shock.—Now though as easy a man you would think as any in the wide world, there was no such thing as making him unsay one of these sort of vows,* which he had learned to reverence when young, as I well remember teaching him to toss up for bog berries on my knee.—So I saw the affair was as good as settled between him and Miss Isabella, and I had no more to say but to wish her joy, which I did the week afterwards upon her return from Scotland with my poor master.

My new lady was young, as might be supposed of a lady that had been carried off by her own consent to Scotland, but I could only see her at the first through her veil, which, from bashfulness or fashion, she kept over her face—'And am I to walk through all this crowd of people, my dearest love?' said she to Sir Condy, meaning us servants and tenants, who had gathered at the back gate—'My dear (said Sir Condy) there's nothing for it but to walk, or to let me carry you as far as the

* *Vows*—It has been maliciously and unjustly hinted, that the lower classes of the people in Ireland pay but little regard to oaths; yet it is certain that some oaths or vows have great power over their minds.—Sometimes they swear they will be revenged on some of their neighbours; this is an oath they never are known to break.—But what is infinitely more extraordinary and unaccountable, they sometimes make a vow against whiskey; these vows are usually limited to a short time.—A woman who has a drunken husband is most fortunate if she can prevail upon him to go to the priest, and make a vow against whiskey for a year, or a month, or a week, or a day.

house, for you see the back road's too narrow for a carriage, and the great piers have tumbled down across the front approach, so there's no driving the right way by reason of the ruins'—'Plato, thou reasonest well!'[36] said she, or words to that effect, which I could no ways understand; and again, when her foot stumbled against a broken bit of a car wheel, she cried out—'Angels and ministers of grace, defend us!'[37]—Well, thought I, to be sure if she's no Jewish like the last, she is a mad woman for certain, which is as bad: it would have been as well for my poor master to have taken up with poor Judy, who is in her right mind any how.

She was dressed like a mad woman, moreover, more than like any one I ever saw afore or since, and I could not take my eyes off her, but still followed behind her, and her feathers on the top of her hat were broke going in at the low back door, and she pulled out her little bottle out of her pocket to smell to when she found herself in the kitchen, and said, 'I shall faint with the heat of this odious, odious place'—'My dear, it's only three steps across the kitchen, and there's a fine air if your veil was up,' said Sir Condy, and with that threw back her veil, so that I had then a full sight of her face; she had not at all the colour of one going to faint, but a fine complexion of her own, as I then took it to be, though her maid told me after it was all put on; but even complexion and all taken in, she was no way, in point of good looks, to compare to poor Judy; and with all she had a quality toss with her; but may be it was my over partiality to

Judy, into whose place I may say she stept, that made me notice all this.—To do her justice, however, she was, when we came to know her better, very liberal in her house-keeping, nothing at all of the Skin-flint in her; she left every thing to the housekeeper, and her own maid, Mrs. Jane, who went with her to Scotland, gave her the best of characters for generosity; she seldom or ever wore a thing twice the same way, Mrs. Jane told us, and was always pulling her things to pieces, and giving them away, never being used in her father's house to think of expence in any thing—and she reckoned, to be sure, to go on the same way at Castle Rackrent; but when I came to enquire, I learned that her father was so mad with her for running off after his locking her up, and forbidding her to think any more of Sir Condy, that he would not give her a farthing; and it was lucky for her she had a few thousands of her own, which had been left to her by a good grandmother, and these were very convenient to begin with. My master and my lady set out in great stile; they had the finest coach and chariot, and horses and liveries, and cut the greatest dash in the county, returning their wedding visits!—and it was immediately reported that her father had undertaken to pay all my master's debts, and of course all his tradesmen gave him a new credit, and every thing went on smack smooth, and I could not but admire my lady's spirit, and was proud to see Castle Rackrent again in all its glory.—My lady had a fine taste for building and furniture, and play-houses, and she turned every thing topsy-turvy, and made the barrack-room into a theatre, as she called it, and she went on as if she had a mint of money at her elbow; and to be sure I thought she knew best, especially as Sir Condy said nothing to it one way or the other. All he asked, God bless him! was to live in peace and quietness, and have his bottle, or his whiskey punch at night to himself.—Now this was little enough, to be sure, for any gentleman, but my lady couldn't abide the smell of the whiskey punch.—'My dear, (says he) you liked it well enough before we were married, and why not now?'—'My dear, (said she) I never smelt it, or I assure you I should never have prevailed upon myself to marry you.'—'My dear, I am sorry you did not smell it, but we can't help that now, (returned my master, without putting himself in a passion, or going out of his way, but just fair and easy helped himself to another glass, and drank it off to her good health). All this the butler told me, who was going backwards and forwards unnoticed with the jug, and hot water, and sugar, and all he thought wanting.—Upon my master's swallowing the last glass of whiskey punch, my lady burst into tears, calling him an ungrateful, base, barbarous wretch! and went off into a fit of hysterics, as I think Mrs. Jane called it, and my poor master was greatly frighted, this being the first thing of the kind he had seen; and he fell straight on his knees before her, and, like a good-hearted cratur as he was, ordered the whiskey punch out of the room, and bid 'em throw open all the windows, and cursed himself, and then my lady came to herself again, and when she saw him kneeling there, bid him get up, and not forswear himself any more, for that she was sure he did not love her, nor never had: this we learnt from Mrs. Jane, who was the only person left present at all this—'My dear, (returns my master, thinking to be sure of Judy, as well he might) whoever told you so is an incendiary, and I'll have 'em turned out of the house this minute, if you'll only let me know which of them it was.'—'Told me what?' says my lady, starting upright in her chair.—'Nothing, nothing at all, (said my master, seeing he had overshot himself, and that my lady spoke at random) but what you said just now that I did not love you, Bella, who told you that?'—'My own sense,' said she, and she put her handkerchief to her face, and leant back upon Mrs. Jane, and fell to sobbing as if her heart would break.—'Why now Bella, this is very strange of you, (said my poor master) if nobody has told you nothing, what is it you are taking on for at this rate,[38] and exposing yourself and me for this way?'—'Oh say no more, say no more, every word you say kills me, (cried my lady, and she ran on like one, as Mrs. Jane says, raving)—Oh Sir Condy, Sir Condy! I that had hoped to find in you "my father, brother, husband, friend".'[39]—'Why now faith this is a little too much; do Bella, try to recollect yourself, my dear; am not I your husband, and of your own chusing, and is not that enough?'—'Oh too much! too much!' cried my lady, wringing her hands.—'Why, my dear, come to your right senses for the love of heaven—see is not the whiskey punch, jug and bowl and all, gone out of the room long ago? what is it in the wide world you have to complain of?'—But still my lady sobbed and sobbed, and called herself the most wretched of women; and among other out of the way provoking things, asked my master, was he fit company for her, and he drinking all night.—This nettling him, which it was hard to do, he replied, that as to drinking all night, he was then as sober as she was herself, and that it was no matter how much a man drank, provided it did no ways affect or stagger him—that as to being fit company for her, he thought himself of a family to be fit company for any lord or lady in the land, but that he never prevented her from seeing and keeping what company she pleased, and that he had done his best to make Castle Rackrent pleasing to her since her marriage, having always had the house full of visitors, and if her own relations were not amongst them, he said, that was their own fault and their pride's fault, of which he was sorry to find her ladyship had so unbecoming a share—So concluding, he took his candle and walked off to his room, and my lady was in her tantarums for three days after, and would have been so much longer, no doubt, but some of her friends, young ladies and cousins and second cousins, came to Castle Rackrent, by my poor master's express invitation, to see her, and she was in a hurry to get up, as Mrs. Jane called it, a play for them, and so got well, and was as finely dressed and as happy to look at as ever, and all the young ladies who used to be in her room dressing of her said in

Mrs. Jane's hearing, that my lady was the happiest bride ever they had seen, and that to be sure a love match was the only thing for happiness, where the parties could any way afford it.

As to affording it, God knows it was little they knew of the matter; my lady's few thousands could not last for ever, especially the way she went on with them, and letters from tradesfolk came every post thick and three-fold, with bills as long as my arm of years and years standing; my son Jason had 'em all handed over to him, and the pressing letters were all unread by Sir Condy, who hated trouble and could never be brought to hear talk of business, but still put it off and put it off, saying—settle it any how, or bid 'em call again to-morrow, or speak to me about it some other time.—Now it was hard to find the right time to speak, for in the mornings he was a-bed and in the evenings over his bottle, where no gentleman chuses to be disturbed.—Things in a twelve-month or so came to such a pass, there was no making a shift to go on any longer, though we were all of us well enough used to live from hand to mouth at Castle Rack-rent. One day, I remember, when there was a power of company, all sitting after dinner in the dusk, not to say dark, in the drawing-room, my lady having rung five times for candles and none to go up, the housekeeper sent up the footman, who went to my mistress and whispered behind her chair how it was.—'My lady, (says he) there are no candles in the house.'—'Bless me, (says she) then take a horse, and gallop off as fast as you can to Carrick O'Fungus and get some.'—'And in the mean time tell them to step into the play-house, and try if there are not some bits left,' added Sir Condy, who happened to be within hearing. The man was sent up again to my lady, to let her know there was no horse to go but one that wanted a shoe.—'Go to Sir Condy, then, I know nothing at all about the horses, (said my lady) why do you plague me with these things?'—How it was settled I really forget, but to the best of my remembrance, the boy was sent down to my son Jason's to borrow candles for the night. Another time in the winter, and on a desperate cold day, there was no turf in for the parlour and above stairs, and scarce enough for the cook in the kitchen, the little *gossoon** was sent off to the neighbours to see and beg or borrow some, but none could he bring back with him for love or money; so as needs must we were forced to trouble Sir Condy—'Well, and if there's no turf to be had in the town or country, why what signifies talking any more about it, can't ye go and cut down a tree?'[40]—'Which tree, please your honor?' I made bold to say.—'Any tree at all that's good to burn, (said Sir Condy); send off smart, and get one down and the fires lighted before my lady gets up to breakfast, or the house will be too hot to hold us.'—He was always

* *Gossoon*—a little boy—from the French word *Garçon*.—In most Irish families there *used* to be a bare-footed Gossoon, who was slave to the cook and the butler, and who in fact, without wages, did all the hard work of the house.—Gossoons were always employed as messengers.—The Editor has known a gossoon to go on foot, without shoes or stockings, fifty-one English miles between sun-rise and sun-set.

very considerate in all things about my lady, and she wanted for nothing whilst he had it to give.—Well, when things were tight with them about this time, my son Jason put in a word again about the lodge, and made a genteel offer to lay down the purchase money to relieve Sir Condy's distresses.—Now Sir Condy had it from the best authority, that there were two writs come down to the Sheriff[41] against his person, and the Sheriff, as ill luck would have it, was no friend of his, and talked how he must do his duty, and how he would do it, if it was against the first man in the county, or even his own brother, let alone one who had voted against him at the last election, as Sir Condy had done.—So Sir Condy was fain to take the purchase money of the lodge from my son Jason to settle matters; and sure enough it was a good bargain for both parties, for my son bought the fee simple of a good house for him and his heirs for ever for little or nothing, and by selling of it for that same my master saved himself from a gaol. Every way it turned out fortunate for Sir Condy; for before the money was all gonc there came a general election, and he being so well beloved in the county, and one of the oldest families, no one had a better right to stand candidate for the vacancy; and he was called upon by all his friends, and the whole county I may say, to declare himself against the old member, who had little thought of a contest. My master did not relish the thoughts of a troublesome canvas, and all the ill will he might bring upon himself by disturbing the peace of the county, besides the expence, which was no trifle; but all his friends called upon one another to subscribe, and formed themselves into a committee, and wrote all his circular letters for him, and engaged all his agents, and did all the business unknown to him, and he was well pleased that it should be so at last, and my lady herself was very sanguine about the election, and there was open house kept night and day at Castle Rackrent, and I thought I never saw my lady look so well in her life as she did at that time; there were grand dinners, and all the gentlemen drinking success to Sir Condy till they were carried off; and then dances and balls, and the ladies all finishing with a raking pot of tea[g] in the morning. Indeed it was well the company made it their choice to sit up all nights, for there was not half beds enough[42] for the sights of people that were in it, though there were shake downs in the drawing-room always made up before sun-rise, for those that liked it. For my part, when I saw the doings that were going on, and the loads of claret that went down the throats of them that had no right to be asking for it, and the sights of meat that went up to table and never came down, besides what was carried off to one or t'other below stairs, I couldn't but pity my poor master who was to pay for all, but I said nothing for fear of gaining myself ill will. The day of election will come some time or other, says I to myself, and all will be over—and so it did, and a glorious day it was as any I ever had the happiness to see; huzza! huzza! Sir Condy Rackrent for ever, was the first thing I hears in the morning, and the same and nothing else all day, and not a soul sober only just when polling, enough to give their votes as became 'em, and to stand the brow-beating of the lawyers who came tight enough upon us; and many of our freeholders were knocked off, having never a freehold that they could safely swear to, and Sir Condy was not willing to have any man perjure himself for his sake, as was done on the other side, God knows, but no matter for that.—Some of our friends were dumb-founded, by the lawyers asking them—had they ever been upon the ground where their freeholds lay?—Now Sir Condy being tender of the consciences of them that had not been on the ground, and so could not swear to a freehold when cross-examined by them lawyers, sent out for a couple of cleaves-full of the sods of his farm of Gulteeshinnagh:[43] and as soon as the sods came into town he set each man upon his sod, and so then ever after, you know, they could fairly swear they had been upon the ground*.—We gained the day by this piece of honesty.[44] I thought I should have died in the streets for joy when I seed my poor master chaired, and he bare-headed and it raining as hard as it could pour; but all the crowds following him up and down, and he bowing and shaking hands with the whole town.—'Is that Sir Condy Rackrent in the chair?' says a stranger man in the crowd—'The same,' says I—who else should it be? God bless him!'—'And I take it then you belong to him,' says he.—'Not at all,' (says I) 'but I live under him, and have done

* This was actually done at an election in Ireland.

so these two hundred years and upwards, me and mine.' —'It's lucky for you, then,' rejoins he, 'that he is where he is, for was he any where else but in the chair this minute he'd be in a worse place, for I was sent down on purpose to put him up*, and here's my order for so doing in my pocket.'—It was a writ that villain the wine merchant had marked against my poor master, for some hundreds of an old debt which it was a shame to be talking of at such a time as this.—'Put it in your pocket again, and think no more of it any ways for seven years to come, my honest friend, (says I), he's a member a Parliament now, praised be God, and such as you can't touch him; and if you'll take a fool's advice, I'd have ye keep out of the way this day, or you'll run a good chance of getting your deserts amongst my master's friends, unless you chuse to drink his health like every body else.'—'I've no objection to that in life,' said he; so we went into one of the public houses kept open for my master, and we had a great deal of talk about this thing and that, and 'how is it (says he) your master keeps on so well upon his legs; I heard say he was off Holantide twelve-month past.'—'Never was better or heartier in his life,' said I.—'It's not that I'm after speaking of, (said he) but there was a great report of his being ruined.' —'No matter, (says I) the Sheriffs two years running were his particular friends, and the Sub-sheriffs were both of them gentlemen, and were properly spoken to; and so the writs lay snug with them, and they, as I

* *To put him up*—to put him in gaol.

understand by my son Jason the custom in them cases is, returned the writs as they came to them to those that sent 'em, much good may it do them, with word in Latin that no such person as Sir Condy Rackrent, Bart. was to be found in those parts.'—'Oh, I understand all those ways better, no offence, than you,' says he, laughing, and at the same time filling his glass to my master's good health, which convinced me he was a warm friend in his heart after all, though appearances were a little suspicious or so at first.—'To be sure, (says he, still cutting his joke) when a man's over head and shoulders in debt, he may live the faster for it and the better if he goes the right way about it—or else how is it so many live on so well, as we see every day, after they are ruined?'—'How is it, (says I, being a little merry at the time) how is it but just as you see the ducks in the kitchen yard just after their heads are cut off by the cook, running round and round faster than when alive.'—At which conceit he fell a laughing, and remarked he had never had the happiness yet to see the chicken yard at Castle Rackrent.—'It won't be long so, I hope, (says I) you'll be kindly welcome there, as every body is made by my master; there is not a freer spoken gentleman or a better beloved, high or low, in all Ireland.'—And of what passed after this I'm not sensible, for we drank Sir Condy's good health and the downfall of his enemies till we could stand no longer ourselves—And little did I think at the time, or till long after, how I was harbouring my poor master's greatest of enemies myself. This fellow had the impudence, after coming to see the chicken-yard, to get me to introduce him to my son Jason—little more than the man that never was born did I guess at his meaning by this visit; he gets him a correct list fairly drawn out from my son Jason of all my master's debts, and goes straight round to the creditors and buys them all up, which he did easy enough, seeing the half of them never expected to see their money out of Sir Condy's hands. Then when this base-minded limb of the law, as I afterwards detected him in being, grew to be sole creditor over all, he takes him out a custodiam[45] on all the denominations and sub-denominations, and every carton and half carton[g] upon the estate—and not content with that, must have an execution against the master's goods and down to the furniture, though little worth, of Castle Rackrent itself.—But this is a part of my story I'm not come to yet, and it's bad to be fore-stalling—ill news flies fast enough all the world over. To go back to the day of the election, which I never think of but with pleasure and tears of gratitude for those good times; after the election was quite and clean over, there comes shoals of people from all parts, claiming to have obliged my master with their votes, and putting him in mind of promises which he could never remember himself to have made—one was to have a freehold for each of his four sons—another was to have a renewal of a lease—another an abatement—one came to be paid ten guineas for a pair of silver buckles sold my master on the hustings, which turned out to be no better than copper gilt—another had a long bill for oats, the half of which never went into the granary to my certain knowledge, and the other half were not fit for the cattle to touch; but the bargain was made the week before the election, and the coach and saddle horses were got into order for the day, besides a vote fairly got by them oats—so no more reasoning on that head—but then there was no end to them that were telling Sir Condy he had engaged to make their sons excisemen, or high constables, or the like; and as for them that had bills to give in for liquor, and beds, and straw, and ribbons, and horses, and post-chaises for the gentlemen freeholders that came from all parts and other counties to vote for my master, and were not, to be sure, to be at any charges, there was no standing against all these; and worse than all the gentlemen of my master's committee, who managed all for him, and talked how they'd bring him in without costing him a penny, and subscribed by hundreds very genteelly, forgot to pay their subscriptions, and had laid out in agents and lawyers, fees and secret service money, the Lord knows how much, and my master could never ask one of them for their subscription, you are sensible, nor for the price of a fine horse he had sold one of them, so it all was left at his door. He could never, God bless him again, I say, bring himself to ask a gentleman for money, despising such sort of conversation himself; but others, who were not gentlemen born, behaved very uncivil in pressing him at this very time, and all he could do to content 'em all was to take himself out of the way as fast as possible to Dublin, where my lady had taken a house as fitting for him, a Member of Parliament, to attend his duty in there all the winters.—I was very lonely when the whole family was gone, and all the things they had ordered to go and forgot sent after them by the stage. There was then a great silence in Castle Rackrent, and I went moping from room to room, hearing the doors clap for want of right locks, and the wind through the broken windows that the glazier never would come to mend, and the rain coming through the roof and best ceilings all over the house, for want of the slater whose bill was not paid; besides our having no slates or shingles for that part of the old building which was shingled, and burnt when the chimney took fire, and had been open to the weather ever since. I took myself to the servants' hall in the evening to smoke my pipe as usual, but missed the bit of talk we used to have there sadly, and ever after was content to stay in the kitchen and boil my little potatoes*, and put up my bed there; and every post day I looked in the newspaper, but no news of my master in the house.—He never spoke good or bad—but, as the butler wrote down word to my son Jason, was very ill used by the government about a place that was promised him and never given, after his supporting them against his conscience very honorably, and being greatly abused for it, which hurt him greatly,

* *My little potatoes*—Thady does not mean by this expression that his potatoes were less than other people's, or less than the usual size—*little* is here used only as an Italian diminutive, expressive of fondness.

he having the name of a great patriot in the country before. The house and living in Dublin too was not to be had for nothing, and my son Jason said Sir Condy must soon be looking out for a new agent, for I've done my part and can do no more—if my lady had the bank of Ireland to spend, it would go all in one winter, and Sir Condy would never gainsay her, though he does not care the rind of a lemon for her all the while.

Now I could not bear to hear Jason giving out after this manner against the family, and twenty people standing by in the street. Ever since he had lived at the Lodge of his own he looked down, howsomever, upon poor old Thady, and was grown quite a great gentleman, and had none of his relations near him—no wonder he was no kinder to poor Sir Condy than to his own kith and kin*. —In the spring it was the villain that got the list of the debts from him brought down the custodiam, Sir Condy still attending his duty in Parliament; and I could scarcely believe my own old eyes, or the spectacles with which I read it, when I was shewn my son Jason's name joined in the custodiam; but he told me it was only for form's sake, and to make things easier, than if all the land was under the power of a total stranger.—Well, I did not know what to think—it was hard to be talking ill of my own, and I could not but grieve for my poor master's fine estate, all torn by these vultures of the law; so I said nothing, but just looked on to see how it would all end.

* *Kith and kin*—family or relations—*Kin* from *kind*—*Kith* from—— we know not what.

It was not till the month of June that he and my lady came down to the country.—My master was pleased to take me aside with him to the brewhouse that same evening, to complain to me of my son and other matters, in which he said he was confident I had neither art nor part: he said a great deal more to me, to whom he had been fond to talk ever since he was my white-headed boy before he came to the estate, and all that he said about poor Judy I can never forget, but scorn to repeat. —He did not say an unkind word of my lady, but wondered, as well he might, her relations would do nothing for him or her, and they in all this great distress.—He did not take any thing long to heart, let it be as it would, and had no more malice or thought of the like in him than the child that can't speak; this night it was all out of his head before he went to his bed.—He took his jug of whiskey punch—My lady was grown quite easy about the whiskey punch by this time, and so I did suppose all was going on right betwixt them, till I learnt the truth through Mrs. Jane, who talked over their affairs to the housekeeper, and I within hearing. The night my master came home, thinking of nothing at all, but just making merry, he drank his bumper toast 'to the deserts of that old curmudgeon my father-in-law, and all enemies at Mount Juliet's town.'—Now my lady was no longer in the mind she formerly was, and did no ways relish hearing her own friends abused in her presence, she said.—'Then why don't they shew themselves your friends, (said my master,) and oblige me with the loan of the money I condescended, by your advice, my dear, to ask?—It's now three posts since I sent off my letter, desiring in the postscript a speedy answer by the return of the post, and no account at all from them yet.'—'I expect they'll write to *me* next post,' says my lady, and that was all that passed then; but it was easy from this to guess there was a coolness betwixt them, and with good cause.

The next morning being post day, I sent off the gossoon early to the post-office to see was there any letter likely to set matters to rights, and he brought back one with the proper post-mark upon it, sure enough, and I had no time to examine, or make any conjecture more about it, for into the servants' hall pops Mrs. Jane with a blue bandbox in her hand, quite entirely mad.—'Dear Ma'am, and what's the matter?' says I.—'Matter enough, (says she) don't you see my band-box is wet through, and my best bonnet here spoiled, besides my lady's, and all by the rain coming in through that gallery window, that you might have got mended if you'd had any sense, Thady, all the time we were in town in the winter.'—'Sure I could not get the glazier, Ma'am,' says I.—'You might have stopped it up any how,' says she.—'So I did, Ma'am, to the best of my ability, one of the panes with the old pillow-case, and the other with a piece of the old stage green curtain—sure I was as careful as possible all the time you were away, and not a drop of rain came in at that window of all the windows in the house, all winter, Ma'am, when under my care;

and now the family's come home, and it's summer time, I never thought no more about it to be sure—but dear, it's a pity to think of your bonnet, Ma'am—but here's what will please you, Ma'am, a letter from Mount Juliet's town for my lady.' With that she snatches it from me without a word more, and runs up the back stairs to my mistress; I follows with a slate to make up the window—this window was in the long passage, or gallery, as my lady gave out orders to have it called, in the gallery leading to my master's bed-chamber and her's, and when I went up with the slate, the door having no lock, and the bolt spoilt, was a-jar after Mrs. Jane, and as I was busy with the window, I heard all that was saying within.

'Well, what's in your letter, Bella, my dear? (says he) you're a long time spelling it over.'—'Won't you shave this morning, Sir Condy,' says she, and put the letter in her pocket.—'I shaved the day before yesterday, (says he) my dear,[46] and that's not what I'm thinking of now—but any thing to oblige you, and to have peace and quietness, my dear'—and presently I had a glimpse of him at the cracked glass over the chimney-piece, standing up shaving himself to please my lady.—But she took no notice, but went on reading her book, and Mrs. Jane doing her hair behind.—'What is it you're reading there, my dear?—phoo, I've cut myself with this razor; the man's a cheat that sold it me, but I have not paid him for it yet—What is it you're reading there? did you hear me asking you, my dear?' 'The sorrows of Werter,'[47] replies my lady, as well as I could hear.—'I think more of the sorrows of Sir Condy, (says my master, joking like).—What news from Mount Juliet's town?'—'No news, (says she) but the old story over again; my friends all reproaching me still for what I can't help now.'—'Is it for marrying me, (said my master, still shaving); what signifies, as you say, talking of that when it can't be helped now.'

With that she heaved a great sigh, that I heard plain enough in the passage.—'And did not you use me basely, Sir Condy, (says she) not to tell me you were ruined before I married you?'—'Tell you, my dear, (said he) did you ever ask me one word about it? and had not you friends enough of your own, that were telling you nothing else from morning to night, if you'd have listened to them slanders.'—'No slanders, nor are my friends slanderers; and I can't bear to hear them treated with disrespect as I do, (says my lady, and took out her pocket handkerchief)—they are the best of friends, and if I had taken their advice—But my father was wrong to lock me up, I own; that was the only unkind thing I can charge him with; for if he had not locked me up, I should never have had a serious thought of running away as I did.'—'Well, my dear, (said my master) don't cry and make yourself uneasy about it now, when it's all over, and you have the man of your own choice in spite of 'em all.'—'I was too young, I know, to make a choice at the time you ran away with me, I'm sure,' says my lady, and another sigh, which made my master, half shaved as he was, turn round upon her in surprise—'Why Bella, (says he) you can't deny what you know as well as I do, that it was at your own particular desire, and that twice under your own hand and seal expressed, that I should carry you off as I did to Scotland, and marry you there.'—'Well, say no more about it, Sir Condy, (said my lady, pettish like)—I was a child then, you know.'—'And as far as I know, you're little better now, my dear Bella, to be talking in this manner to your husband's *face*; but I won't take it ill of you, for I know it's something in that letter you put in your pocket just now, that has set you against me all on a sudden, and imposed upon your understanding.'—'It is not so very easy as you think it, Sir Condy, to impose upon *my* understanding', (said my lady)—'My dear, (says he) I have, and with reason, the best opinion of your understanding of any man now breathing, and you know I have never set my own in competition with it; till now, my dear Bella, (says he, taking her hand from her book as kind as could be,) till now—when I have the great advantage of being quite cool, and you not; so don't believe one word your friends say against your own Sir Condy, and lend me the letter out of your pocket, till I see what it is they can have to say.'—'Take it then, (says she,) and as you are quite cool, I hope it is a proper time to request you'll allow me to comply with the wishes of all my own friends, and return to live with my father and family, during the remainder of my wretched existence, at Mount Juliet's Town.'

At this my poor master fell back a few paces, like one that had been shot—'You're not serious, Bella, (says he) and could you find it in your heart to leave me this way in the very middle of my distresses, all alone?'—But recollecting himself after his first surprise, and a moment's time for reflection, he said, with a great deal of consideration for my lady—'Well, Bella, my dear, I believe you are right; for what could you do at Castle Rackrent, and an execution against the goods coming down, and the furniture to be canted, and an auction in the house all next week—so you have my full consent to go, since that is your desire, only you must not think of my accompanying you, which I could not in honour do upon the terms I always have been since our marriage with your friends; besides I have business to transact at home—so in the mean time, if we are to have any breakfast this morning, let us go down and have it for the last time in peace and comfort, Bella.'

Then as I heard my master coming to the passage door, I finished fastening up my slate against the broken pane, and when hc came out, I wiped down the window seat with my wig*, bade him a good morrow as kindly

* Wigs were formerly used instead of brooms in Ireland, for sweeping or dusting tables, stairs, &c. The Editor doubted the fact, till he saw a labourer of the old school sweep down a flight of stairs with his wig; he afterwards put it on his head again with the utmost composure, and said, 'Oh please your honour, it's never a bit the worse.'

It must be acknowledged that these men are not in any danger of catching cold by taking off their wigs occasionally, because they usually have fine crops of hair growing under their wigs.—The wigs are often yellow, and the hair which appears from beneath them black; the wigs are usually too small, and are raised up by the hair beneath, or by the ears of the wearers.

as I could, seeing he was in trouble, though he strove and thought to hide it from me.—'This window is all racked and tattered, (says I,) and it's what I'm striving to mend.' 'It *is* all racked and tattered plain enough, (says he) and never mind mending it, honest old Thady, says he, it will do well enough for you and I, and that's all the company we shall have left in the house by-and-bye.'—'I'm sorry to see your honour so low this morning, (says I,) but you'll be better after taking your breakfast.'—'Step down to the servants' hall, (says he) and bring me up the pen and ink into the parlour, and get a sheet of paper from Mrs. Jane, for I have business that can't brook to be delayed, and come into the parlour with the pen and ink yourself, Thady, for I must have you to witness my signing a paper I have to execute in a hurry.'—Well, while I was getting of the pen and ink-horn, and the sheet of paper, I ransacked my brains to think what could be the papers my poor master could have to execute in such a hurry, he that never thought of such a thing as doing business afore breakfast in the whole course of his life for any man living—but this was for my lady, as I afterwards found, and the more genteel of him after all her treatment.

I was just witnessing the paper that he had scrawled over, and was shaking the ink out of my pen upon the carpet, when my lady came in to breakfast, and she started as if it had been a ghost, as well she might, when she saw Sir Condy writing at this unseasonable hour.—'That will do very well, Thady,' says he to me, and took the paper I had signed to, without knowing what upon the earth it might be, out of my hands, and walked, folding it up, to my lady—

'You are concerned in this, my lady Rackrent, (says he, putting it into her hands,) and I beg you'll keep this memorandum safe, and shew it to your friends the first thing you do when you get home, but put it in your pocket now, my dear, and let us eat our breakfast, in God's name.'—'What is all this?' said my lady, opening the paper in great curiosity—'It's only a bit of a memorandum of what I think becomes me to do whenever I am able, (says my master); you know my situation, tied hand and foot at the present time being, but that can't last always, and when I'm dead and gone, the land will be to the good, Thady, you know; and take notice it's my intention your lady should have a clear five hundred a year jointure off the estate, afore any of my debts are paid.'—'Oh, please your honour, says I, I can't expect to live to see that time, being now upwards of fourscore and ten years of age, and you a young man, and likely to continue so, by the help of God.'—I was vexed to see my lady so insensible too, for all she said was—'This is very genteel of you, Sir Condy—You need not wait any longer, Thady'—so I just picked up the pen and ink that had tumbled on the floor, and heard my master finish with saying—'You behaved very genteel to me, my dear, when you threw all the little you had in your own power, along with yourself, into my hands; and as I don't deny but what you may have had some things to complain of, (to be sure he was thinking then of Judy, or of the whiskey punch, one or t'other, or both); and as I don't deny but you may have had something to complain of, my dear, it is but fair you should have something in the form of compensation to look forward too agreeably in future; besides it's an act of justice to myself, that none of your friends, my dear, may ever have it to say against me I married for money, and not for love.'—'That is the last thing I should ever have thought of saying of you, Sir Condy,' said my lady, looking very gracious.—'Then, my dear, (said Sir Condy) we shall part as good friends as we met, so, all's right.'

I was greatly rejoiced to hear this, and went out of the parlour to report it all to the kitchen.—The next morning my lady and Mrs. Jane set out for Mount Juliet's town in the jaunting car; many wondered at my lady's chusing to go away, considering all things, upon the jaunting car, as if it was only a party of pleasure; but they did not know till I told them, that the coach was all broke in the journey down, and no other vehicle but the car to be had; besides, my lady's friends were to send their coach to meet her at the cross roads—so it was all done very proper.

My poor master was in great trouble after my lady left us.—The execution came down, and every thing at Castle Rackrent was seized by the gripers,[48] and my son Jason, to his shame be it spoken, amongst them—I wondered, for the life of me, how he could harden himself to do it, but then he had been studying the law, and had made himself attorney Quirk; so he brought down at once a heap of accounts upon my master's head—To Cash lent, and to ditto, and to ditto, and to ditto, and oats, and bills paid at the milliner's and linen-draper's, and many dresses for the fancy balls in Dublin for my lady, and all the bills to the workmen and tradesmen for the scenery of the theatre, and the chandler's and grocer's bills, and taylor's, besides butcher's and baker's, and worse than all, the old one of that base wine-merchant's, that wanted to arrest my poor master for the amount on the election day, for which amount Sir Condy afterwards passed his note of hand, bearing lawful interest from the date thereof; and the interest and compound interest was now mounted to a terrible deal on many other notes and bonds for money borrowed, and there was besides hush-money to the sub-sheriffs, and sheets upon sheets of old and new attornies' bills, with heavy balances, *as per former account furnished*, brought forward with interest thereon; then there was a powerful deal due to the Crown for sixteen years arrear of quit-rent[49] of the town lands of Carrickshaughlin, with drivers' fees, and a compliment to the receiver every year for letting the quit-rent run on, to oblige Sir Condy and Sir Kit afore him.—Then there was bills for spirits, and ribbons at the election time, and the gentlemen of the Committee's accounts unsettled, and their subscriptions never gathered; and there was cows to be paid for, with the smith and farrier's bills to be set against the rent of the demesne, with calf and hay-money: then there was all the servants' wages, since I don't know when, coming due to them, and sums advanced for them by my son Jason for clothes, and boots, and whips, and odd monies for sundries expended by them in journies to town and elsewhere, and pocket-money for the master continually, and messengers and postage before his being a parliament man—I can't myself tell you what besides; but this I know, that when the evening came on the which Sir Condy had appointed to settle all with my son Jason; and when he comes into the parlour, and sees the sight of bills and load of papers all gathered on the great dining table for him, he puts his hands before both his eyes, and cries out—'Merciful Jasus! what is it I see before me!'—Then I sets an arm chair at the table for him, and with a deal of difficulty he sits him down, and my son Jason hands him over the pen and ink to sign to this man's bill and t'other man's bill, all which he did without making the least objections; indeed, to give him his due, I never seen a man more fair, and honest, and easy in all his dealings, from first to last, as Sir Condy, or more willing to pay every man his own as far as he was able, which is as much as any one can do.—'Well, (says he, joking like with Jason) I wish we could settle it all with a stroke of my grey-goose-quill.—What signifies making me wade through all this ocean of papers here; can't you now, who understand drawing out an account, Debtor and Creditor, just sit down here at the corner of the table, and get it done out for me, that I may have a clear view of the balance, which is all I need be talking about, you know?'—'Very true, Sir Condy, nobody understands business better than yourself,' says Jason.—'So I've a right to do, being born and bred to the bar, (says Sir Condy)—Thady, do step out and see are they bringing in the tings[50] for the punch, for we've just done all we have to do this evening.'—I goes out accordingly, and when I came back, Jason was pointing to the balance, which was a terrible sight to my poor master.—'Pooh! pooh! pooh! (says he) here's so many noughts they dazzle my eyes, so they do, and put me in mind of all I suffered, larning of my numeration table, when I was a boy, at the day-school along with you, Jason—Units, tens, hundreds, tens of hundreds.—Is the punch ready, Thady?' says he, seeing me—'Immediately, the boy has the jug in his hand; it's coming up stairs, please your honour, as fast as possible,' says I, for I saw his honour was tired out of his life, but Jason, very short and cruel, cuts me off with—'Don't be talking of punch yet a while, it's no time for punch yet a bit—Units, tens, hundreds, goes he on, counting over the master's shoulder—units, tens, hundreds, thousands'—'A-a-agh! hold your hand, (cries my master,) where in this wide world am I to find hundreds, or units itself, let alone thousands?' —'The balance has been running on too long, (says Jason, sticking to him as I could not have done at the time if you'd have given both the Indies and Cork to boot); the balance has been running on too long, and I'm distressed myself on your account, Sir Condy, for money, and the thing must be settled now on the spot, and the balance cleared off,' says Jason. 'I'll thank you, if you'll only shew me how,' says Sir Condy.—'There's but one way, (says Jason) and that's ready enough; when there's no cash, what can a gentleman do but go to the land?'—'How can you go to the land, and it under custodiam to yourself already, (says Sir Condy) and another custodiam hanging over it? and no one at all can touch it, you know, but the custodees.'—'Sure can't you sell, though at a loss?—sure you can sell, and I've a purchaser ready for you,' says Jason.—'Have ye so? (said Sir Condy) that's a great point gained; but there's a thing now beyond all, that perhaps you don't know yet, barring Thady has let you into the secret.'—'Sarrah[51] bit of a sacret, or any thing at all of the kind has he learned from me these fifteen weeks come St. John's eve, (says I) for we have scarce been upon speaking terms of late—but what is it your honor means of a secret?'—'Why the secret of the little keepsake I gave my lady Rackrent the morning she left us, that she might not go back empty-handed to her friends.'—'My lady Rackrent, I'm sure, has baubles and keepsakes enough, as those bills on the table will shew, (says Jason); but whatever it is, (says he, taking up his pen) we must add it to the balance, for to be sure it can't be paid for.'—'No, nor can't till after my decease, (said Sir Condy) that's one good thing.'—Then coloring up a good deal, he tells Jason of the memorandum of the five hundred a year jointure he had settled upon my lady; at which Jason was indeed mad, and said a great deal in very high words, that it was using a gentleman who had the management of his affairs, and was moreover his principal creditor, extremely ill, to do such a thing without consulting him, and against his knowledge and consent. To all which Sir Condy had nothing to reply, but that, upon his conscience, it was in a hurry, and without a moment's thought on his part, and he was very sorry for it, but if it was to do over again he would do the same; and he appealed to me, and I was ready to give my evidence, if that would do, to the truth of all he said.

So Jason with much ado was brought to agree to a compromise.—'The purchaser that I have ready (says he) will be much displeased to be sure at the incumbrance on the land, but I must see and manage him—here's a deed ready drawn up—we have nothing to do but to put in the consideration money and our names to it.—And how much am I going to sell?—the lands of O'Shaughlin's-town, and the lands of Gruneaghoolaghan, and the lands of Crookaghnawaturgh, (says he, just reading to himself)—and—'Oh, murder, Jason!—sure you won't put this in'—the castle, stable, and appurtenances of Castle Rackrent—Oh, murder! (says I, clapping my hands) this is too bad, Jason.'—'Why so? (said Jason) when it's all, and a great deal more to the back of it, lawfully mine was I to push for it.' 'Look at him (says I, pointing to Sir Condy, who was just leaning back in his arm chair, with his arms falling beside him like one stupified) is it you, Jason, that can stand in his presence and recollect all he has been to us, and all we have been to him, and yet use him so at the last?'—'Who will he find to use him better, I ask you? (said Jason)—If he can get a better purchaser, I'm content; I only offer to purchase to make things easy and oblige him—though I don't see what compliment I am under, if you come to that; I have never had, asked, or charged more than sixpence in the pound receiver's fees, and where would he have got an agent for a penny less?' 'Oh Jason! Jason! how will you stand to this in the face of the county, and all who know you, (says I); and what will people tink[52] and say, when they see you living here in Castle Rackrent, and the lawful owner turned out of the seat of his ancestors, without a cabin to put his head into, or so much as a potatoe to eat?'—Jason, whilst I was saying this and a great deal more, made me signs, and winks, and frowns; but I took no heed, for I was grieved and sick at heart for my poor master, and couldn't but speak.

'Here 's the punch! (says Jason, for the door opened) —here 's the punch!'—Hearing that, my master starts up in his chair and recollects himself, and Jason uncorks the whiskey—'Set down the jug here,' says he, making room for it beside the papers opposite to Sir Condy, but still not stirring the deed that was to make over all. Well, I was in great hopes he had some touch of mercy about him, when I saw him making the punch, and my master took a glass; but Jason put it back as he was going to fill again, saying, 'No, Sir Condy, it shan't be said of me, I got your signature to this deed when you were half-seas over; you know, your name and hand-writing in that condition would not, if brought before the courts, benefit me a straw, wherefore let us settle all before we go deeper in the punch-bowl.'—'Settle all as you will, (said Sir Condy, clapping his hands to his ears) but let me hear no more, I'm bothered to death this night.'—'You've only to sign,' said Jason, putting the pen to him.—'Take all and be content,' said my master—So he signed—and the man who brought in the punch witnessed it, for I was not able, but crying like a child; and besides, Jason said, which I was glad of, that I was no fit witness, being so old and doating. It was so bad with me, I could not taste a drop of the punch itself, though my master himself, God bless him! in the midst of his trouble, poured out a glass for me and brought it up to my lips.—'Not a drop, I thank your honor's honor as much as if I took it though,' and I just set down the glass as it was and went out; and when I got to the street door, the neighbour's childer who were playing at marbles there, seeing me in great trouble, left their play, and gathered about me to know what ailed me; and I told them all, for it was a great relief to me to speak to these poor childer, that seemed to have some natural feeling left in them: and when they were made sensible that Sir Condy was going to leave Castle Rackrent for good and all, they set up a whillalu that could be heard to the farthest end of the street; and one fine boy he was, that my master had given an apple to that morning, cried the loudest, but they all were the same sorry, for Sir Condy was greatly beloved amongst the childer* for letting them go a nutting in the demesne without saying a word to them, though my lady objected to them.—The people in the town who were the most of them standing at their doors, hearing the childer cry, would know the reason of it; and when the report was made known, the people one and all gathered in great anger against my son Jason, and terror at the notion of his coming to be landlord over them, and they cried, No Jason! No Jason!—Sir Condy! Sir Condy! Sir Condy Rackrent for ever! and the mob grew so great and so loud I was frighted, and made my way back to the house to warn my son to make his escape, or hide himself for fear of the consequences.—Jason would not believe me, till they came all round the house and to the windows with great shouts—then he grew quite pale, and asked Sir Condy what had he best do?—'I'll tell you what you'd best do, (said Sir Condy, who was laughing to see his fright) finish your glass first, then let's go to the window and shew ourselves, and I'll tell 'em, or you shall if you please, that I'm going to the Lodge for change of air for my health, and by my own desire, for the rest of my days.'—'Do so,' said Jason, who never meant it should have been so, but could not refuse him the Lodge at this unseasonable time. Accordingly Sir Condy threw up the sash and explained matters, and thanked all his friends, and bid 'em look in at the punch bowl, and observe that Jason and he had been sitting over it very good friends; so the mob was

* This is the invariable pronunciation of the lower Irish.[53]

content, and he sent 'em out some whiskey to drink his health, and that was the last time his honor's health was ever drank at Castle Rackrent.

The very next day, being too proud, as he said to me, to stay an hour longer in a house that did not belong to him, he sets off to the Lodge, and I along with him not many hours after. And there was great bemoaning through all O'Shaughlin's town, which I stayed to witness, and gave my poor master a full account of when I got to the Lodge. —He was very low and in his bed when I got there, and complained of a great pain about his heart, but I guessed it was only trouble, and all the business, let alone vexation, he had gone through of late; and knowing the nature of him from a boy, I took my pipe, and while smoking it by the chimney, began telling him how he was beloved and regretted in the county, and it did him a deal of good to hear it.—'Your honor has a great many friends yet that you don't know of, rich and poor, in the county (says I); for as I was coming along on the road I met two gentlemen in their own carriages, who asked after you, knowing me, and wanted to know where you was, and all about you, and even how old I was—think of that.'—Then he wakened out of his doze, and began questioning me who the gentlemen were. And the next morning it came into my head to go, unknown to any body, with my master's compliments round to many of the gentlemen's houses where he and my lady used to visit, and people that I knew were his great friends, and would go to Cork to serve him any day in the year, and

I made bold to try to borrow a trifle of cash from them.—They all treated me very civil for the most part, and asked a great many questions very kind about my lady and Sir Condy and all the family, and were greatly surprised to learn from me Castle Rackrent was sold, and my master at the Lodge for his health; and they all pitied him greatly, and he had their good wishes if that would do, but money was a thing they unfortunately had not any of them at this time to spare. I had my journey for my pains, and I, not used to walking, nor supple as formerly, was greatly tired, but had the satisfaction of telling my master when I got to the Lodge all the civil things said by high and low.

'Thady, (says he) all you've been telling me brings a strange thought into my head; I've a notion I shall not be long for this world any how, and I've a great fancy to see my own funeral afore I die.' I was greatly shocked at the first speaking to hear him speak so light about his funeral, and he to all appearance in good health, but recollecting myself, answered—'To be sure it would be a fine sight as one could see, I dared to say, and one I should be proud to witness, and I did not doubt his honor's would be as great a funeral as ever Sir Patrick O'Shaughlin's was, and such a one as that had never been known in the county afore or since.' But I never thought he was in earnest about seeing his own funeral himself, till the next day he returns to it again.—'Thady, (says he) as far as the wake* goes, sure I might without any great trouble

* A wake[g] in England is a meeting avowedly for merriment—in Ireland, it is a nocturnal meeting avowedly for the purpose of watching and bewailing the dead; but in reality for gossipping and debauchery.

have the satisfaction of seeing a bit of my own funeral.'— 'Well, since your honor's honor's so bent upon it, (says I, not willing to cross him, and he in trouble) we must see what we can do.'—So he fell into a sort of a sham disorder, which was easy done, as he kept his bed and no one to see him; and I got my shister, who was an old woman very handy about the sick, and very skilful, to come up to the Lodge to nurse him; and we gave out, she knowing no better, that he was just at his latter end, and it answered beyond any thing; and there was a great throng of people, men, women and childer, and there being only two rooms at the Lodge, except what was locked up full of Jason's furniture and things, the house was soon as full and fuller than it could hold, and the heat, and smoke, and noise wonderful great; and standing amongst them that were near the bed, but not thinking at all of the dead, I was started by the sound of my master's voice from under the great coats that had been thrown all at top, and I went close up, no one noticing.— 'Thady, (says he) I've had enough of this, I'm smothering, and I can't hear a word of all they're saying of the deceased.'—'God bless you, and lie still quiet (says I) a bit longer, for my shister's afraid of ghosts, and would die on the spot with the fright, was she to see you come to life all on a sudden this way without the least preparation.'—So he lays him still, though well nigh stifled, and I made all haste to tell the secret of the joke, whispering to one and t'other, and there was a great surprise, but not so great as we had laid out it would.—'And aren't we to have the pipes and tobacco, after coming so far to-night?' says some; but they were all well enough pleased when his honor got up to drink with them, and sent for more spirits from a shebean-house*, where they very civilly let him have it upon credit—so the night passed off very merrily, but to my mind Sir Condy was rather upon the sad order in the midst of it all, not finding there had been such a great talk about himself after his death as he had always expected to hear.

The next morning when the house was cleared of them, and none but my shister and myself left in the kitchen with Sir Condy, one opens the door and walks in, and who should it be but Judy M'Quirk herself.—I forgot to notice that she had been married long since, whilst young Captain Moneygawl lived at the Lodge, to the Captain's huntsman, who after a while listed and left her, and was killed in the wars. Poor Judy fell off greatly in her good looks after her being married a year or two, and being smoke-dried in the cabin and neglecting herself like, it was hard for Sir Condy himself to know her again till she spoke; but when she says, 'It's Judy M'Quirk, please your honor, don't you remember her?'—'Oh, Judy, is it you? (says his honor)—yes, sure I remember you very well—but you're greatly altered, Judy.'—'Sure it's time for me, (says she) and I think your honor since I *seen* you last, but that's a great while ago, is altered too.'—'And with reason, Judy, (says Sir

* ***Shebean-house***, a hedge alehouse.—Shebean properly means weak small-beer, taplash.[54]

Condy, fetching a sort of sigh)—but how's this, Judy, (he goes on) I take it a little amiss of you that you were not at my wake last night?' 'Ah, don't be being jealous of that, (says she) I didn't hear a sentence of your honor's wake till it was all over, or it would have gone hard with me but I would have been at it sure—but I was forced to go ten miles up the country three days ago to a wedding of a relation of my own's, and didn't get home till after the wake was over; but (says she) it won't be so, I hope, the next time*, please your honor.'—'That we shall see, Judy, (says his honor) and may be sooner than you think for, for I've been very unwell this while past, and don't reckon any way I'm long for this world.' At this Judy takes up the corner of her apron, and puts it first to one eye and then to t'other, being to all appearance in great trouble; and my shister put in her word, and bid his honor have a good heart, for she was sure it was only the gout that Sir Patrick used to have flying about him, and that he ought to drink a glass or a bottle extraordinary to keep it out of his stomach, and he promised to take her advice, and sent out for more spirits immediately; and Judy made a sign to me, and I went over to the door to her, and she said—'I wonder to see Sir Condy so low!—Has he heard the news?' 'What news?' says I. —'Didn't ye hear it, then? (says she) my lady Rackrent that was is kilt[g] and lying for dead, and I don't doubt but it's all over with her by this time.'—'Mercy on us all,

* At the coronation of one of our monarchs, the king complained of the confusion which happened in the procession—The great officer who presided told his majesty, 'That it should not be so next time.'

(says I) how was it?'—'The jaunting car it was that that ran away with her, (says Judy).—I was coming home that same time from Biddy M'Guggin's marriage, and a great crowd of people too upon the road coming from the fair of Crookaghnawatur, and I sees a jaunting car standing in the middle of the road, and with the two wheels off and all tattered.—What's this? says I.'—'Didn't ye hear of it? (says they that were looking on) it's my lady Rackrent's car that was running away from her husband, and the horse took fright at a carrion that lay across the road, and so ran away with the jaunting car, and my lady Rackrent and her maid screaming, and the horse ran with them against a car that was coming from the fair, with the boy asleep on it, and the lady's petticoat hanging out of the jaunting car caught, and she was dragged I can't tell you how far upon the road, and it all broken up with the stones just going to be pounded, and one of the road makers with his sledge hammer in his hand stops the horse at the last; but my lady Rackrent was all kilt* and smashed, and they lifted her into a cabin hard by, and the maid was found after, where she had been thrown, in the gripe of the ditch, her cap and bonnet all full of bog water—and they say

* *Kilt and smashed*—Our author is not here guilty of an anticlimax.—The mere English reader, from a similarity of sound between the words *kilt* and *killed*, might be induced to suppose that their meanings are similar, yet they are not by any means in Ireland synonymous terms. Thus you may hear a man exclaim—'I'm kilt and murdered!'—but he frequently means only that he has received a black eye, or a slight contusion.—*I'm kilt all over*—means that he is in a worse state than being simply *kilt*—Thus—*I'm kilt with the cold*—is nothing to—*I'm kilt all over with the rheumatism.*[g]

my lady can't live any way. Thady, pray now is it true what I'm told for sartain, that Sir Condy has made over all to your son Jason?'—'All,' says I.—'All entirely,' says she again.—'All entirely,' says I.—'Then (says she) that's a great shame, but don't be telling Jason what I say.'—'And what is it you say? (cries Sir Condy, leaning over betwixt us, which made Judy start greatly)—I know the time when Judy M'Quirk would never have stayed so long talking at the door, and I in the house.' 'Oh, (says Judy) for shame, Sir Condy, times are altered since then, and it's my lady Rackrent you ought to be thinking of.'—'And why should I be thinking of her, that's not thinking of me now?' says Sir Condy.—'No matter for that, (says Judy, very properly) it's time you should be thinking of her if ever you mean to do it at all, for don't you know she's lying for death?'—'My lady Rackrent! (says Sir Condy in a surprise) why it's but two days since we parted, as you very well know, Thady, in her full health and spirits, and she and her maid along with her going to Mount Juliet's town on her jaunting car.'—'She'll never ride no more on her jaunting car, (said Judy) for it has been the death of her sure enough.'—'And is she dead then?' says his honor.—'As good as dead, I hear, (says Judy) but there's Thady here has just learnt the whole truth of the story as I had it, and it is fitter he or any body else should be telling it you than I, Sir Condy—I must be going home to the childer.'—But he stops her, but rather from civility in him, as I could see very plainly, than any thing else, for Judy was, as his honor remarked, at her first coming in, greatly changed, and little likely, as far as I could see—though she did not seem to be clear of it herself—little likely to be my lady Rackrent now, should there be a second toss-up to be made.—But I told him the whole story out of the face, just as Judy had told it to me, and he sent off a messenger with his compliments to Mount Juliet's town that evening to learn the truth of the report, and Judy bid the boy that was going call in at Tim M'Enerney's shop in O'Shaughlin's town and buy her a new shawl.—'Do so, (says Sir Condy) and tell Tim to take no money from you, for I must pay him for the shawl myself.'—At this my shister throws me over a look, and I says nothing, but turned the tobacco in my mouth, whilst Judy began making a many words about it, and saying how she could not be beholden for shawls to[55] any gentleman. I left her there to consult with my shister, did she think there was any thing in it, and my shister thought I was blind to be asking her the question, and I thought my shister must see more into it than I did, and recollecting all past times and every thing, I changed my mind, and came over to her way of thinking, and we settled it that Judy was very like to be my lady Rackrent after all, if a vacancy should have happened.

The next day, before his honor was up, somebody comes with a double knock at the door, and I was greatly surprised to see it was my son Jason.—'Jason, is it you? (says I) what brings you to the Lodge? (says I) is it my lady Rackrent? we know that already since yesterday.'

'May be so, (says he) but I must see Sir Condy about it.' —'You can't see him yet, (says I) sure he is not awake.' 'What then, (says he) can't he be wakened? and I standing at the door.'—'I'll not be disturbing his honor for you, Jason (says I); many's the hour you've waited in your time, and been proud to do it, till his honor was at leisure to speak to you.—His honor,' says I, raising my voice—at which his honor wakens of his own accord, and calls to me from the room to know who it was I was speaking to. Jason made no more ceremony, but follows me into the room.—'How are you, Sir Condy, (says he) I'm happy to see you looking so well; I came up to know how you did to-day, and to see did you want for any thing at the Lodge.'—'Nothing at all, Mr. Jason, I thank you, (says he, for his honor had his own share of pride, and did not chuse, after all that had passed, to be beholden, I suppose, to my son)—but pray take a chair and be seated, Mr. Jason.'—Jason sat him down upon the chest, for chair there was none, and after he had sat there some time, and a silence on all sides—'What news is there stirring in the country, Mr. Jason M'Quirk?' says Sir Condy, very easy, yet high like.—'None that's news to you, Sir Condy, I hear (says Jason) I am sorry to hear of my lady Rackrent's accident.'—'I am much obliged to you, and so is her ladyship, I'm sure,' answers Sir Condy, still stiff; and there was another sort of a silence, which seemed to lie the heaviest on my son Jason.

'Sir Condy, (says he at last, seeing Sir Condy disposing

himself to go to sleep again) Sir Condy, I dare say you recollect mentioning to me the little memorandum you gave to lady Rackrent about the £500 a year jointure.'—'Very true, (said Sir Condy) it is all in my recollection.'—'But if my lady Rackrent dies there's an end of all jointure,' says Jason. 'Of course,' says Sir Condy.—'But it's not a matter of certainty that my lady Rackrent won't recover,' says Jason.—'Very true, Sir,' says my master.—'It's a fair speculation then, for you to consider what the chance of the jointure on those lands when out of custodiam will be to you.'—'Just five hundred a year, I take it, without any speculation at all,' said Sir Condy.—'That's supposing the life dropt and the custodiam off, you know, begging your pardon, Sir Condy, who understand business, that is a wrong calculation.'—'Very likely so, (said Sir Condy) but Mr. Jason, if you have any thing to say to me this morning about it, I'd be obliged to you to say it, for I had an indifferent night's rest last night, and wouldn't be sorry to sleep a little this morning.'—'I have only three words to say, and those more of consequence to you, Sir Condy, than me. You are a little cool, I observe, but I hope you will not be offended at what I have brought here in my pocket,'—and he pulls out two long rolls, and showers down golden guineas upon the bed. 'What's this? (said Sir Condy) it's long since'—but his pride stops him—'All these are your lawful property this minute, Sir Condy, if you please,' said Jason.—'Not for nothing, I'm sure, (said Sir Condy, and laughs a little)—nothing for nothing, or

I'm under a mistake with you, Jason.'—'Oh, Sir Condy, we'll not be indulging ourselves in any unpleasant retrospects, (says Jason) it's my present intention to behave, as I'm sure you will, like a gentleman in this affair.—Here's two hundred guineas, and a third I mean to add, if you should think proper to make over to me all your right and title to those lands that you know of.'—'I'll consider of it,' said my master; and a great deal more, that I was tired listening to, was said by Jason, and all that, and the sight of the ready cash upon the bed worked with his honor; and the short and the long of it was, Sir Condy gathered up the golden guineas and tied up in a handkerchief, and signed some paper Jason brought with him as usual, and there was an end of the business; Jason took himself away, and my master turned himself round and fell asleep again.

I soon found what had put Jason in such a hurry to conclude this business. The little gossoon we had sent off the day before with my master's compliments to Mount Juliet's town, and to know how my lady did after her accident, was stopped early this morning, coming back with his answer through O'Shaughlin's town, at Castle Rackrent by my son Jason, and questioned of all he knew of my lady from the servants at Mount Juliet's town; and the gossoon told him my lady Rackrent was not expected to live over night, so Jason thought it high time to be moving to the Lodge, to make his bargain with my master about the jointure afore it should be too late, and afore the little gossoon should reach us with the news. My master was greatly vexed, that is, I may say, as much as ever I seen him, when he found how he had been taken in; but it was some comfort to have the ready cash for immediate consumption in the house any way.

And when Judy came up that evening, and brought the childer to see his honor, he unties the handkerchief, and God bless him! whether it was little or much he had, 'twas all the same with him, he gives 'em all round guineas a-piece.—'Hold up your head, (says my shister[56] to Judy, as Sir Condy was busy filling out a glass of punch for her eldest boy)—Hold up your head, Judy, for who knows but we may live to see you yet at the head of the Castle Rackrent estate.'—'May be so, (says she) but not the way you are thinking of.'—I did not rightly understand which way Judy was looking when she makes this speech, till a while after.—'Why Thady, you were telling me yesterday that Sir Condy had sold all entirely to Jason, and where then does all them guineas in the handkerchief come from?' 'They are the purchase money of my lady's jointure,' says I.—Judy looks a little bit puzzled at this.—'A penny for your thoughts, Judy, (says my shister)—hark, sure Sir Condy is drinking her health.'—He was at the table in *the room*,* drinking with the exciseman and the gauger,[57] who came up to see his honor, and we were standing over the fire in the kitchen.—'I don't much care is he drinking my health or not (says Judy), and it is not Sir Condy I'm thinking of, with all your jokes, whatever he is of me.' 'Sure you

* *The room*—the principal room in the house.

wouldn't refuse to be my lady Rackrent, Judy, if you had the offer?' says I.—'But if I could do better?' says she. 'How better?' says I and my shister both at once.—'How better! (says she) why what signifies it to be my lady Rackrent and no Castle? sure what good is the car and no horse to draw it?'—'And where will ye get the horse, Judy?' says I.—'Never you mind that, (says she)—may be it is your own son Jason might find that.'—'Jason! (says I) don't be trusting to him, Judy. Sir Condy, as I have good reason to know, spoke well of you, when Jason spoke very indifferently of you, Judy.'—'No matter (says Judy), it's often men speak the contrary just to what they think of us.'—'And you the same way of them, no doubt, (answers I).—Nay don't be denying it, Judy, for I think the better of ye for it, and shouldn't be proud to call ye the daughter of a shister's son of mine, if I was to hear ye talk ungrateful, and any way disrespectful of his honor.'—'What disrespect, (says she) to say I'd rather, if it was my luck, be the wife of another man?' 'You'll have no luck, mind my words, Judy,' says I; and all I remembered about my poor master's goodness in tossing up for her afore he married at all came across me, and I had a choaking in my throat that hindered me to say more.—'Better luck, any how, Thady, (says she) than to be like some folk, following the fortunes of them that have none left.' 'Oh King of Glory! (says I) hear the pride and ungratitude of her, and he giving his last guineas but a minute ago to her childer, and she with the fine shawl on her he made her a present of but yesterday!'—'Oh troth, Judy, you're wrong now,' says my shister, looking at the shawl.—'And was not he wrong yesterday then, (says she) to be telling me I was greatly altered, to affront me?'—'But Judy, (says I) what is it brings you here then at all in the mind you are in—is it to make Jason think the better of you?'—'I'll tell you no more of my secrets, Thady, (says she) nor would havc told you this much, had I taken you for such an unnatural fader as I find you are, not to wish your own son prefarred to another.'—'Oh troth, *you* are wrong, now, Thady,' says my shister.—Well, I was never so put to it in my life between these womens, and my son and my master, and all I felt and thought just now, I could not upon my conscience tell which was the wrong from the right.—So I said not a word more, but was only glad his honor had not the luck to hear all Judy had been saying of him, for I reckoned it would have gone nigh to break his heart, not that I was of opinion he cared for her as much as she and my shister fancied, but the ungratitude of the whole from Judy might not plase him, and he could never stand the notion of not being well spoken of or beloved like behind his back. Fortunately for all parties concerned, he was so much elevated at this time, there was no danger of his understanding any thing, even if it had reached his ears. There was a great horn at the Lodge, ever since my master and Captain Moneygawl was in together, that used to belong originally to the celebrated Sir Patrick, his ancestor, and his honor was fond often of telling the story that he larned from me when a child, how Sir Patrick drank the full of this horn without stopping, and this was what no other man afore or since could without drawing breath.—Now Sir Condy challenged the gauger, who seemed to think little of the horn, to swallow the contents, and it filled to the brim, with punch; and the gauger said it was what he could not do for nothing, but he'd hold Sir Condy a hundred guineas he'd do it.—'Done, (says my master) I'll lay you a hundred golden guineas to a tester* you don't.'—'Done,' says the gauger, and done and done's enough between two gentlemen. The gauger was cast, and my master won the bet, and thought he'd won a hundred guineas, but by the wording it was adjudged to be only a tester that was his due, by the exciseman. It was all one to him, he was as well pleased, and I was glad to see him in such spirits again.

The gauger, bad luck to him! was the man that next proposed to my master to try himself could he take at a draught the contents of the great horn.—'Sir Patrick's horn! (said his honor) hand it to me—I'll hold you your own bet over again I'll swallow it.'—'Done, (says the gauger) I'll lay ye any thing at all you do no such thing.'—'A hundred guineas to sixpence I do, (says he) bring me the handkerchief.'—I was loth, knowing he meant the handkerchief with the gold in it, to bring it out

* *Tester*—Sixpence—from the French word tête, a head. A piece of silver stamped with a head, which in old French was called, 'un testion,' and which was about the value of an old English sixpence.—Tester is used in Shakspeare.[58]

in such company, and his honor not very well able to reckon it. 'Bring me the handkerchief then, Thady,' says he, and stamps with his foot; so with that I pulls it out of my great coat pocket, where I had put it for safety.—Oh, how it grieved me to see the guineas counting upon the table, and they the last my master had. Says Sir Condy to me—'Your hand is steadier than mine to-night, Old Thady, and that's a wonder; fill you the horn for me.'—And so wishing his honor success, I did—but I filled it, little thinking of what would befall him.—He swallows it down, and drops like one shot.—We lifts him up, and he was speechless and quite black in the face. We put him to bed, and in a short time he wakened raving with a fever on his brain. He was shocking either to see or hear.—'Judy! Judy! have ye no touch of feeling? won't you stay to help us nurse him?' says I to her, and she putting on her shawl to go out of the house.—'I'm frighted to see him, (says she) and wouldn't, nor couldn't stay in it—and what use?—he can't last till the morning.' With that she ran off.—There was none but my shister and myself left near him of all the many friends he had. The fever came and went, and came and went, and lasted five days, and the sixth he was sensible for a few minutes, and said to me, knowing me very well—'I'm in burning pain all within side of me, Thady,'—I could not speak, but my shister asked him, would he have this thing or t'other to do him good?—'No, (says he) nothing will do me good no more'—and he gave a terrible screech with the torture he was in—then again a minute's ease—'brought to this by drink (says he)—where are all the friends?—where's Judy?—Gone, hey?—Aye, Sir Condy has been a fool all his days'—said he, and there was the last word he spoke, and died. He had but a very poor funeral, after all.

If you want to know any more, I'm not very well able to tell you; but my lady Rackrent did not die as was expected of her, but was only disfigured in the face ever after by the fall and bruises she got; and she and Jason, immediately after my poor master's death, set about going to law about that jointure; the memorandum not being on stamped paper, some say it is worth nothing, others again it may do; others say, Jason won't have the lands at any rate—many wishes it so—for my part, I'm tired wishing for any thing in this world, after all I've seen in it—but I'll say nothing; it would be a folly to be getting myself ill will in my old age. Jason did not marry, nor think of marrying Judy, as I prophesied, and I am not sorry for it—who is?—As for all I have here set down from memory and hearsay of the family, there's nothing but truth in it from beginning to end, that you may depend upon, for where's the use of telling lies about the things which every body knows as well as I do?

The Editor could have readily made the catastrophe of Sir Condy's history more dramatic and more pathetic, if he thought it allowable to varnish the plain round tale of faithful Thady. He lays it before the English reader as a specimen of manners and characters, which are perhaps unknown in England. Indeed the domestic habits of no nation in Europe were less known to the English than those of their sister country, till within these few years.

Mr. Young's picture of Ireland,[59] in his tour through that country, was the first faithful portrait of its inhabitants. All the features in the foregoing sketch were taken from the life, and they are characteristic of that mixture of quickness, simplicity, cunning, carelessness, dissipation, disinterestedness, shrewdness and blunder, which in different forms, and with various success, has been brought upon the stage or delineated in novels.

It is a problem of difficult solution to determine, whether an Union[60] will hasten or retard the amelioration of this country. The few gentlemen of education who now reside in this country will resort to England: they are few, but they are in nothing inferior to men of the same rank in Great Britain. The best that can happen will be the introduction of British manufacturers in their places.

Did the Warwickshire militia,[61] who were chiefly artisans, teach the Irish to drink beer, or did they learn from the Irish to drink whiskey?[62]

ADVERTISEMENT
TO THE
ENGLISH READER

SOME friends who have seen Thady's history since it has been printed[63] have suggested to the Editor, that many of the terms and idiomatic phrases with which it abounds could not be intelligible to the English reader without farther explanation. The Editor has therefore furnished the following Glossary.

GLOSSARY[64]

Page 7. *Monday morning*] Thady begins his Memoirs of the Rackrent Family by dating *Monday morning*, because no great undertaking can be auspiciously commenced in Ireland on any morning but *Monday morning*.—'Oh, please God we live till Monday morning, we'll set the slater to mend the roof of the house—On Monday morning we'll fall to and cut the turf—On Monday morning we'll see and begin mowing—On Monday morning, please your honor, we'll begin and dig the potatoes,' &c.

All the intermediate days between the making of such speeches and the ensuing Monday are wasted, and when Monday morning comes it is ten to one that the business is deferred to *the next* Monday morning. The Editor knew a gentleman who, to counteract this prejudice, made his workmen and laborers begin all new pieces of work upon a Saturday.

Page 9. Let alone the three kingdoms itself] *Let alone*, in this sentence, means *put out of the consideration*. This phrase *let alone*, which is now used as the imperative of a verb, may in time become a conjunction, and may exercise the ingenuity of some future etymologist. The celebrated Horne Tooke has proved most satisfactorily, that the conjunction *but* comes from the imperative of the Anglo-Saxon verb (*beonutan*) *to be out*; also that *if* comes from *gif*, the imperative of the Anglo-Saxon verb which signifies *to give*, &c. &c.

Page 11. Whillaluh] Ullaloo, Gol, or lamentation over the dead—

'Magnoque ululante tumultu.' VIRGIL.

'Ululatibus omne
Implevere nemus.' OVID.

A full account of the Irish Gol or Ullaloo, and of the Caoinan or Irish funeral song, with its first semichorus, second semichorus, full chorus of sighs and groans, together with the Irish words and music, may be found in the fourth volume of the Transactions of the Royal Irish Academy. For the advantage of *lazy* readers, who would rather read a page than walk a yard, and from compassion, not to say sympathy with their infirmity, the Editor transcribes the following passages.

'The Irish have been always remarkable for their funeral lamentations, and this peculiarity has been noticed by almost every traveller who visited them. And it seems derived from their Celtic ancestors, the primæval inhabitants of this isle. . . .'

'It has been affirmed of the Irish, that to cry was more natural to them than to any other nation, and at length the Irish cry became proverbial. . . .'

'Cambrensis in the twelfth century says, the Irish then musically expressed their griefs; that is, they applied the musical art, in which they excelled all others, to the orderly celebration of funeral obsequies, by dividing the mourners into two bodies, each alternately singing their part, and the whole at times joining in full chorus. . . . The body of the deceased, dressed in grave clothes and ornamented with flowers, was placed on a bier or some elevated spot. The relations and Keeners (*singing mourners*) ranged themselves in two divisions, one at the head and the other at the feet of the corpse. The bards and croteries had before prepared the funeral Caoinan. The chief bard of the head chorus began by singing the first stanza in a low, doleful tone, which was softly accompanied by the harp: at the conclusion the foot semichorus began the lamentation, or Ullaloo, from the final note of the preceding stanza, in which they were answered by the head semichorus; then both united in one general chorus. The chorus of the first stanza being ended, the chief bard of the foot semichorus began the second Gol or lamentation, in which they were answered by that of the head;[64a] and then as before both united in the general full chorus. Thus alternately were the song and chorusses performed during the night. The genealogy, rank, possessions, the virtues and vices of the dead were rehearsed, and a number of interrogations were addressed to the deceased: as,

Why did he die? If married, whether his wife was faithful to him, his sons dutiful, or good hunters or warriors? If a woman, whether her daughters were fair or chaste? If a young man, whether he had been crossed in love? or if the blue-eyed maids of Erin treated him with scorn?'

We are told that formerly the feet (the metrical feet) of the Caoinan were much attended to, but on the decline of the Irish bards these feet were gradually neglected, the Caoinan fell into a sort of slip-shod metre amongst women. Each province had different Caoinans, or at least different imitations of the original. There was the Munster cry, the Ulster cry, &c. It became an extempore performance, and every set of Keeners varied the melody according to their own fancy.

It is curious to observe how customs and ceremonies degenerate. The present Irish cry or howl cannot boast of much melody, nor is the funeral procession conducted with much dignity. The crowd of people who assemble at these funerals sometimes amounts to a thousand, often to four or five hundred. They gather as the bearers of the hearse proceed on their way, and when they pass through any village, or when they come near any houses, they begin to cry—Oh! Oh! Oh! Oh! Oh! Agh! Agh! raising their notes from the first *Oh!* to the last *Agh!* in a kind of mournful howl. This gives notice to the inhabitants of the village that a *funeral is passing*, and immediately they flock out to follow it. In the province of Munster it is a common thing for the women to follow a funeral, to join in the universal cry with all their might and main for some time, and then to turn and ask—'Arrah! who is it that's dead?—who is it we're crying for?'—Even the poorest people have their own burying-places, that is, spots of ground in the church-yards, where they say that their ancestors have been buried ever since the wars of Ireland: and if these burial-places are ten miles from the place where a man dies, his friends and neighbours take care to carry his corpse thither. Always one priest, often five or six priests, attend these funerals; each priest repeats a mass, for which he is paid sometimes a shilling, sometimes half a crown, sometimes half a guinea, or a guinea, according to the circumstances, or as they say, according to the *ability* of the deceased. After the burial of any very poor man who has left a widow or children, the priest makes what is called *a collection* for the widow; he goes round to every person present, and each contributes sixpence or a shilling, or what they please. The reader will find in the note upon the word *Wake* more particulars respecting the conclusion of the Irish funerals.

Certain old women, who cry particularly loud and well, are in great request, and, as a man said to the Editor, 'Every one would wish and be proud to have such at his funeral, or at that of his friends.' The lower Irish are wonderfully eager to attend the funerals of their friends and relations, and they make their relationships branch out to a great extent. The proof that a poor man has been well beloved during his life, is his having a crowded funeral. To attend a neighbour's funeral is a cheap proof of humanity, but it does not, as some imagine, cost nothing. The time spent in attending funerals may be safely valued at half a million to the Irish nation: the Editor thinks that double that sum would not be too high an estimate. The habits of profligacy and drunkenness which are acquired at *wakes* are here put out of the question. When a labourer, a carpenter, or a smith is not at his work, which frequently happens, ask where he is gone, and ten to one the answer is—'Oh faith, please your honor, he couldn't do a stroke to-day, for he's gone to *the* funeral.'

Even beggars, when they grow old, go about begging *for their own funerals*; that is, begging for money to buy a coffin, candles, pipes and tobacco.—For the use of the candles, pipes and tobacco, see *Wake*.

Those who value customs in proportion to their antiquity, and nations in proportion to their adherence to antient customs, will doubtless admire the Irish *Ullaloo*, and the Irish nation, for persevering in this usage from time immemorial. The Editor, however, has observed some alarming symptoms, which seem to prognosticate the declining taste for the Ullaloo in Ireland. In a comic theatrical entertainment represented not long since on the Dublin stage, a chorus of old women was introduced, who set up the Irish howl round the relics of a physician, who is supposed to have fallen under the wooden sword of Harlequin. After the old women have continued their Ullaloo for a decent time, with all the necessary accompaniments of wringing their hands, wiping or rubbing their eyes with the corners of their gowns or aprons, &c. one of the mourners suddenly suspends her lamentable cries, and turning to her neighbour, asks—'Arrah now, honey, who is it we're crying for?'

Page 12. The tenants were sent away without their whiskey] It is usual with some landlords to give their inferior tenants a glass of whiskey when they pay their rents. Thady calls it *their* whiskey; not that the whiskey is actually the property of the tenants, but that it becomes their *right*, after it has been often given to them. In this general mode of reasoning respecting *rights*, the lower Irish are not singular, but they are peculiarly quick and tenacious in claiming these rights.—'Last year your honor gave me some straw for the roof of my house, and I *expect* your honor will be after doing the same this year.'—In this manner gifts are frequently turned into tributes. The high and low are not always dissimilar in their habits. It is said that the Sublime Ottoman Porte is very apt to claim gifts as tributes: thus it is dangerous to send the Grand Seignor a fine horse on his birth-day one year, lest on his next birth-day he should expect a similar present, and should proceed to demonstrate the reasonableness of his expectations.

He demeaned himself greatly] Means, he lowered, or disgraced himself much.

Page 14. Duty fowls—and duty turkies—and duty geese] In many leases in Ireland, tenants were *formerly* bound to supply an inordinate quantity of poultry to their landlords. The Editor knew of sixty turkies[65] being reserved in one lease of a small farm.

English tenants] An English tenant does not mean a tenant who is an Englishman, but a tenant who pays his rent the day that it is due. It is a common prejudice in Ireland, amongst the poorer classes of people, to believe that all tenants in England pay their rents on the very day when they become due. An Irishman, when he goes to take a farm, if he wants to prove to his landlord that he is a substantial man, offers to become an *English tenant*. If a tenant disobliges his landlord by voting against him, or against his opinion, at an election, the tenant is immediately informed by the agent that he must become *an English tenant*. This threat does not imply that he is to change his language or his country, but that he must pay all the arrear of rent which he owes, and that he must thenceforward pay his rent on the day when it becomes due.

Canting] Does not mean talking or writing hypocritical nonsense, but selling substantially by auction.

Pages 14–15. Duty work] It was formerly common in Ireland to insert clauses in leases, binding tenants to furnish their landlords with laborers and horses for several days in the year. Much petty tyranny and oppression have resulted from this feudal custom. Whenever a poor man disobliged his landlord, the agent sent to him for his duty work, and Thady does not exaggerate when he says, that the tenants were often called from their own work to do that of their landlord. Thus the very means of earning their rent were taken from them: whilst they were getting home their landlord's harvest, their own was often ruined, and yet their rents were expected to be paid as punctually as if their time had been at their own disposal. This appears the height of absurd injustice.

In Esthonia, amongst the poor Sclavonian race of peasant slaves, they pay tributes to their lords, not under the name of duty work, duty geese, duty turkies, &c. but under the name of *righteousnesses*. The following ballad is a curious specimen of Estonian poetry:

> This is the cause that the country is ruined,
> And the straw of the thatch is eaten away,
> The gentry are come to live in the land—
> Chimneys between the village,
> And the proprietor upon the white floor!
> The sheep brings forth a lamb with a white forehead;
> This is paid to the lord for a *righteousness sheep*.
> The sow farrows pigs,
> They go to the spit of the lord.
> The hen lays eggs,
> They go into the lord's frying-pan.
> The cow drops a male calf,
> That goes into the lord's herd as a bull.
> The mare foals a horse foal,
> That must be for my lord's nag.
> The boor's wife has sons,
> They must go to look after my lord's poultry.

Page 15. Out of forty-nine suits which he had, he never lost one—but seventeen] Thady's language in this instance is a specimen of a mode of rhetoric common in Ireland. An astonishing assertion is made in the beginning of a sentence, which ceases to be in the least surprizing when you hear the qualifying explanation that follows. Thus a man who is in the last stage of staggering drunkenness will, if he can articulate, swear to you—'Upon his conscience now (and may he never stir from the spot alive if he is telling a lie) upon his conscience he has not tasted a drop of any thing, good or bad, since morning at-all at all but half a pint of whiskey, please your honor.'

Page 16. Fairy Mounts] Barrows. It is said that these high mounts were of great service to the natives of Ireland, when Ireland was invaded by the Danes. Watch was always kept on them, and upon the approach of an enemy a fire was lighted to give notice to the next watch, and thus the intelligence was quickly communicated through the country. *Some years ago*, the common people believed that these Barrows were inhabited by fairies, or as they call them, by the *good people*.—'Oh troth, to the best of my belief, and to the best of my judgment and opinion, (said an elderly man to the Editor) it was only the old people that had nothing to do, and got together and were telling stories about them fairies, but to the best of my judgment there's nothing in it.—Only this I heard myself not very many years back, from a decent kind of a man, a grazier, that as he was coming just *fair and easy* (*quietly*) from the fair, with some cattle and sheep that he had not sold, just at the church of ——, at an angle of the road like, he was met by a good looking man, who asked him where was he going? And he answered, "Oh, far enough, I must be going all night."—"No, that you mustn't nor won't (says the man), you'll sleep with me the night, and you'll want for nothing, nor your cattle nor sheep neither, nor your *beast* (*horse*); so come along with me."—With that the grazier *lit* (alighted) from his horse, and it was dark night; but presently he finds himself, he does not know in the wide world how, in a fine house, and plenty of every thing to eat and drink—nothing at all wanting that he could wish for or think of—And he does not *mind* (*recollect*, or *know*) how at last he falls asleep; and in the morning he finds himself lying, not in ever a bed or a house at all, but just in the angle of the road where first he met the strange man: there he finds himself lying on his back on the grass, and all his sheep feeding as quiet as ever all round about him, and his horse the same way, and the bridle of the beast over his wrist. And I asked him what he thought of it, and from first to last he could think of nothing but for certain sure it must have been the fairies that entertained him so well. For there was no house to see any where nigh hand, or any building, or barn, or place at all, but only the church and the *mote* (*barrow*). There's another odd thing enough that they tell about this same church, that if any person's corpse, that had not a right to be buried in that church-yard, went to be burying there in it, no not all the men, women, or childer in all Ireland could get the corpse any way into the church-yard; but as they would be trying to go into the church-yard, their feet would seem to be going backwards instead of forwards; aye, continually backwards the whole funeral would seem to go; and they would never set foot with the corpse in the church-yard. Now they say, that it is the fairies do all this; but it is my opinion it is all idle talk, and people are after being wiser now.'

The country people in Ireland certainly *had* great admiration mixed with reverence, if not dread of fairies. They believed, that beneath these fairy mounts were spacious subterraneous palaces inhabited by *the good people*, who must not on any account be disturbed. When the wind raises a little eddy of dust upon the road, the poor people believe that it is raised by the fairies, that it is a sign that they are journeying from one of the fairy mounts to another, and they say to the fairies, or to the dust as it passes—'God speed ye, gentlemen, God speed ye.' This averts any evil that *the good people* might be inclined to do them. There are innumerable stories told of the friendly and unfriendly feats of these busy fairies; some of these tales are ludicrous, and some romantic enough for poetry. It is a pity that poets should lose such convenient, though diminutive machinery.—By the by, Parnell, who shewed himself so deeply 'skilled of faerie lore,' was an Irishman; and though he has presented his faeries to the world in the ancient English dress of 'Britain's Isle, and Arthur's days,' it is probable that his first acquaintance with them began in his native country.

Some remote origin for the most superstitious or romantic popular illusions or vulgar errors may often be discovered. In Ireland, the old churches and church-yards have been usually fixed upon as the scenes of wonders. Now the antiquarians tell us, that near the ancient churches in that kingdom caves of various constructions have from time to time been discovered, which were formerly used as granaries or magazines by the ancient inhabitants, and as places to which they retreated in time of danger. There is (p. 84 of the R. I. A. Transactions for 1789) a particular account of a number of these artificial caves at the West end of the church of Killossy, in the county of Kildare. Under a rising ground, in a dry sandy soil, these subterraneous dwellings were found: they have pediment roofs, and they communicate with each other by small apertures. In the Brehon laws these are mentioned, and there are fines inflicted by those laws upon persons who steal from the subterraneous granaries. All these things shew, that there was a real foundation for the stories which were told of the appearance of lights and of the sounds of voices near these places. The persons who had property concealed there very willingly countenanced every wonderful relation that tended to make these places objects of sacred awe or superstitious terror.

Page 17. Weed-ashes] By antient usage in Ireland, all the weeds on a farm belonged to the farmer's wife, or to the wife of the squire who holds the ground in his own hands. The great demand for alkaline salts in bleaching rendered these ashes no inconsiderable perquisite.

Sealing-money] Formerly it was the custom in Ireland for tenants to give the squire's lady from two to fifty guineas as a perquisite upon the sealing of their leases. The Editor not very long since knew of a baronet's lady accepting fifty guineas as sealing money, upon closing a bargain for a considerable farm.

Page 18. Sir Murtagh grew mad] Sir Murtagh grew angry.

The whole kitchen was out on the stairs] Means that all the inhabitants of the kitchen came out of the kitchen and stood upon the stairs. These, and similar expressions, shew how much the Irish are disposed to metaphor and amplification.

Page 21. Fining down the yearly rent] When an Irish gentleman, like Sir Kit Rackrent, has lived beyond his income, and finds himself distressed for want of ready money,[66] tenants obligingly offer to take his land at a rent far below the value, and to pay him a small sum of money in hand, which they call fining down the yearly rent. The temptation of this ready cash often blinds the landlord to his future interest.

Driver] A man who is employed to drive tenants for rent; that is, to drive the cattle belonging to tenants to pound. The office of driver is by no means a sinecure.

Page 22. I thought to make him a priest] It was customary amongst those of Thady's rank, in Ireland, whenever they could get a little money, to send their sons abroad to St. Omer's, or to Spain, to be educated as priests. Now they are educated at Maynooth.[67] The Editor has lately known a young lad, who began by being a post-boy, afterwards turn into a carpenter; then quit his plane and work-bench to study his *Humanities*, as he said, at the college of Maynooth: but after he had gone through his course of Humanities, he determined to be a soldier instead of a priest.

Page 25. Flam] Short for flambeau.

Page 26. Barrack room] Formerly it was customary, in gentlemen's houses in Ireland, to fit up one large bedchamber with a number of beds for the reception of occasional visitors. These rooms were called Barrack rooms.

Page 27. An innocent] in Ireland, means a simpleton, an idiot.

Page 35. The Curragh] is the Newmarket of Ireland.

The Cant] The auction.

Page 40. And so should cut him off for ever, by levying a fine, and suffering a recovery to dock the entail][68] The English reader may perhaps be surprised at the extent of Thady's legal knowledge, and at the fluency with which he pours forth law terms; but almost every poor man in Ireland, be he farmer, weaver, shopkeeper, or steward, is, beside his other occupations, occasionally a lawyer. The nature of processes, ejectments, custodiams, injunctions, replevins, &c. &c. are perfectly known to them, and the terms are as familiar to them as to any attorney. They all love law. It is a kind of lottery, in which every man, staking his own wit or cunning against his richer neighbour's[69] property, feels that he has little to lose and much to gain.

'I'll have the law of you, so I will!'—is the saying of an Englishman who expects justice. 'I'll have you before his honor'—is the threat of an Irishman who hopes for partiality. Miserable is the life of a justice of the peace in Ireland the day after a fair, especially if he resides near a small town. The multitude of the *kilt* (*kilt* does not mean *killed*, but hurt) and wounded who come before his honor with black eyes or bloody heads is astonishing, but more astonishing is the number of those, who, though they are scarcely able by daily labour to procure daily food, will nevertheless, without the least reluctance, waste six or seven hours of the day lounging in the yard or hall of a justice of the peace, waiting to make some complaint about—nothing. It is impossible to convince them that *time is money*. They do not set any value upon their own time, and they think that others estimate theirs at less than nothing. Hence they make no scruple of telling a justice of the peace a story of an hour long about a *tester* (sixpence): and if he grow impatient, they attribute it to some secret prejudice which he entertains against them.

Their method is to get a story completely by heart, and to tell it, as they call it, *out of the face*, that is, from the beginning to the end, without interruption.

'Well, my good friend, I have seen you lounging about these three hours in the yard; what is your business?'

'Please your honor, it is what I want to speak one word to your honor.'

'Speak then, but be quick—What is the matter?'

'Nothing strange—The matter,[70] please your honor, is nothing at-all-at-all, only just about the grazing of a horse, please your honor, that this man here sold me at the fair of Gurtishannon last Shrove fair, which lay down three times with myself, please your honor, and *kilt* me; not to be telling your honor of how, no later back than yesterday night, he lay down in the house there within, and all the childer standing round, and it was God's mercy he did not fall a'-top of them, or into the fire to burn himself. So please your honor, to-day I took him back to this man, which owned him, and after a great deal to do I got the mare again I *swopped* (*exchanged*) him for; but he wont't pay the grazing of the horse for the time I had him, though he promised to pay the grazing in case the horse didn't answer; and he never did a day's work, good or bad, please your honor, all the time he was with me, and I had the doctor to him five times, any how. And so, please your honor, it is what I expect your honor will stand my friend, for I'd sooner come to your honor for justice than to any other in all Ireland. And so I brought him here before your honor, and expect your honor will make him pay me the grazing, or tell me, can I process him for it at the next assizes, please your honor?'

The defendant now, turning a quid of tobacco with his tongue into some secret cavern in his mouth, begins his defence with—

'Please your honor, under favor, and saving your honor's presence, there's not a word of truth in all this man has been saying from beginning to end, upon my conscience, and I wouldn't for the value of the horse itself, grazing and all, be after telling your honor a lie. For please your honor, I have a dependance upon your honor that you'll do me justice, and not be listening to him or the like of him. Please your honor, it's what he has brought me before your honor, because he had a spite against me about some oats I sold your honor, which he was jealous of, and a shawl his wife got at my shister's shop there without, and never paid for; so I offered to set the shawl against the grazing, and give him a receipt in full of all demands, but he wouldn't out of spite, please your honor; so he brought me before your honor, expecting your honor was mad with me for cutting down the tree in the horse park, which was none of my doing, please your honor—ill luck to them that went and belied me to your honor behind my back!—So if your honor is pleasing, I'll tell you the whole truth about the horse that he swopped against my mare, out of the face.—Last Shrove fair I met this man, Jemmy Duffy, please your honor, just at the corner of the road where the bridge is broke down that your honor is to have the presentment for this year—long life to you for it!—And he was at that time coming from the fair of Gurtishannon, and I the same way. 'How are you, Jemmy?' says I.—'Very well, I thank ye kindly,

Bryan,' says he; 'shall we turn back to Paddy Salmon's, and take a naggin of whiskey to our better acquaintance?'—'I don't care if I did, Jemmy,' says I; 'only it is what I can't take the whiskey, because I'm under an oath against it for a month.' Ever since, please your honor, the day your honor met me on the road, and observed to me I could hardly stand I had taken so much—though upon my conscience your honor wronged me greatly that same time—ill luck to them that belied me behind my back to your honor!—Well, please your honor, as I was telling you, as he was taking the whiskey, and we talking of one thing or t'other, he makes me an offer to swop his mare that he couldn't sell at the fair of Gurtishannon, because nobody would be troubled with the beast, please your honor, against my horse, and to oblige him I took the mare—sorrow take her! and him along with her!—She kicked me a new car, that was worth three pounds ten, to tatters the first time ever I put her into it, and I expect your honor will make him pay me the price of the car, any how, before I pay the grazing, which I've no right to pay at-all-at-all, only to oblige him.—But I leave it all to your honor—and the whole grazing he ought to be charging for the beast is but two and eight-pence half-penny, any how, please your honor. So I'll abide by what your honor says, good or bad. I'll leave it all to your honor.'

I'll leave *it* all to your honor—literally means, I'll leave all the trouble to your honor.

The Editor knew a justice of the peace in Ireland, who had such a dread of *having it all left to his honor*, that he frequently gave the complainants the sum about which they were disputing to make peace between them, and to get rid of the trouble of hearing their stories *out of the face*. But he was soon cured of this method of buying off disputes, by the increasing multitude of those who, out of pure regard to his honor, came 'to get justice from him, because they would sooner come before him than before any man in all Ireland.'

Page 55. A raking pot of tea] We should observe, that this custom[71] has long since been banished from the higher orders of Irish gentry. The mysteries of a raking pot of tea, like those of the Bona Dea, are supposed to be sacred to females, but now and then it has happened that some of the male species, who were either more audacious or more highly favored than the rest of their sex, have been admitted by stealth to these orgies. The time when the festive ceremony begins varies according to circumstances, but it is never earlier than twelve o'clock at night; the joys of a raking pot of tea depending on its being made in secret, and at an unseasonable hour. After a ball, when the more discreet part of the company had departed to rest, a few chosen female spirits, who have footed it till they can foot it no longer, and till the sleepy notes expire under the slurring hand of the musician, retire to a bed-chamber, call the favorite maid, who alone is admitted, bid her *put down the kettle*, lock the door, and amidst as much giggling and scrambling as possible, they get round a tea-table, on which all manner of things are huddled together. Then begin mutual railleries and mutual confidences amongst the young ladies, and the faint scream and the loud laugh is heard, and the romping for letters and pocket-books begins, and gentlemen are called by their surnames, or by the general name of fellows—pleasant fellows! charming fellows! odious fellows! abominable fellows!—and then all prudish decorums are forgotten, and then we might be convinced how much the satyrical poet was mistaken when he said,

'There is no woman where there's no reserve.'

The merit of the original idea of a raking pot of tea evidently belongs to the washerwoman and the laundry-maid. But why should not we have *Low life above stairs*, as well as *High life below stairs*?

Page 59. Carton, or half Carton] Thady means cartron or half cartron. 'According to the old record in the black book of Dublin, a *cantred* is said to contain 30 *villatas terras*, which are also called *quarters* of land (quarterons, *cartrons*); every one of which quarters must contain so much ground as will pasture 400 cows and 17 plough-lands. A knight's fee was composed of 8 hydes, which amount to 160 acres, and that is generally deemed about a *plough-land*.'

The Editor was favored by a learned friend with the above Extract, from a MS. of Lord Totness's in the Lambeth library.

Page 81. Wake] A wake, in England, means a festival held upon the anniversary of the Saint of the parish. At these wakes rustic games, rustic conviviality, and rustic courtship, are pursued with all the ardour and all the appetite, which accompany such pleasures as occur but seldom.—In Ireland a wake is a midnight meeting, held professedly for the indulgence of holy sorrow, but usually it is converted into orgies of unholy joy. When an Irish man or woman of the lower order dies, the straw which composed his bed, whether it has been contained in a bag to form a mattress, or simply spread upon the earthen floor, is immediately taken out of the house, and burned before the cabin door, the family at the same time setting up the death howl. The ears and eyes of the neighbours being thus alarmed, they flock to the house of the deceased, and by their vociferous sympathy excite and at the same time sooth the sorrows of the family.

It is curious to observe how good and bad are mingled in human institutions. In countries which were thinly inhabited, this custom prevented private attempts against the lives of individuals, and formed a kind of Coroner's inquest upon the body which had recently expired, and burning the straw upon which the sick man lay became a simple preservative against infection. At night the dead body is waked, that is to say, all the friends and neighbours of the deceased collect in a barn or stable, where the corpse is laid upon some boards, or an unhinged door supported upon stools, the face exposed, the rest of the body covered with a white sheet. Round the body are stuck in brass candlesticks, which have been borrowed perhaps at five miles distance, as many candles as the poor person can beg or borrow, observing always to have an odd number. Pipes and tobacco are first distributed, and then according to the *ability* of the deceased, cakes and ale, and sometimes whiskey, are *dealt* to the company.

> 'Deal on, deal on, my merry men all,
> Deal on your cakes and your wine,
> For whatever is dealt at her funeral to-day
> Shall be dealt to-morrow at mine.'

After a fit of universal sorrow, and the comfort of a universal dram, the scandal of the neighbourhood, as in higher circles, occupy the company. The young lads and lasses romp with one another, and when the fathers and mothers are at last overcome with sleep and whiskey, (*vino & somno*) the youth become more enterprizing and are frequently successful. It is said that more matches are made at wakes than at weddings.

Page 84. Kilt] This word frequently occurs in the following pages, where it means not ***killed***, but much ***hurt***. In Ireland, not only cowards, but the brave 'die many times before their death'. There *Killing is no murder*.[72]

APPENDIX

MARIA EDGEWORTH AND TURGENEV

SCOTT's influence upon Ivan Turgenev (1818–83) is well attested. It has long been believed, in addition, that the Russian novelist was influenced by Scott's own source, the Irish novels of Maria Edgeworth. This would be a momentous fact of literary history, if true, especially since the influence is said to date from Turgenev's first book, *A Sportsman's Sketches*, written partly in Paris in 1847–50 and first collected in 1852—the book which, as Turgenev believed in later life, had led Tsar Alexander II to free the serfs in 1861.

The source of this legend of Irish influence is unique and scarcely known—an anonymous obituary of Turgenev in the *Daily News* of 7 September 1883, four days after the novelist's death near Paris. Though now forgotten, the article passed into the currency of literary history by being quoted in part by Thackeray's eldest daughter, Anne Ritchie, in her study of women novelists, *A Book of Sibyls* (1883), where a quotation from it was added in the proofs of the book as a footnote (p. 140 n.). The obituary, which is ignored by Turgenev's biographers, is entitled 'Turguéneff: By One Who Knew Him', and offers a number of intimate details about the novelist's appearance and conversation. The following passage on his literary sources has not been reprinted since 1883:

Turguéneff was the youngest of three very distinguished brothers. Were the eldest of the trio now living he would be almost a centenarian. He remembered Bonaparte, Bernardin [de] St. Pierre, Talleyrand, Sir Walter Scott, of whom he was for some weeks a guest at Abbotsford, Miss Edgeworth when she was in the zenith of her fame; visited Madame de Staël at Coppet, and fell in with Byron as he was making a tour on the Rhine. The eldest Turguéneff was a many-sided man, though not a professional author. He had great literary qualities. . . . When he grew up he made wide incursions into English literature, and came to the conclusion that Maria Edgeworth had struck on a vein which most of the great novelists of the future would exclusively work. She took the world as she found it and selected from it the materials that she thought would be interesting to write about, in a clear and natural style. It was Ivan Turguéneff himself who told me this, and he modestly said that he was an unconscious disciple of Miss Edgeworth in setting out on his literary career. He had not the advantage of knowing English. But as a youth he used to hear his brother translate to visitors at his country house in the Uralian hills passages from 'Irish Tales and Sketches', which he thought superior to her three-volume novels. Turguéneff also said to me, 'It is possible, nay probable, that if Maria Edgeworth had not written about the poor Irish of the co. Longford and the squires and squirees, that it would not have occurred to me to give a literary form to my impressions about the classes parallel to him [them?] in Russia. My brother used, in pointing out the beauties of her unambitious works, to call attention to their extreme simplicity and to the distinction with which she treated the simple ones of the earth.'

The claim of literary influence is unsupported in Turgenev's published letters, where Maria Edgeworth is nowhere mentioned. Nor do Turgenev's novels offer any clear influence of a direct debt. It must be admitted, too, that the obituary is inaccurate on several points. Ivan Turgenev, the novelist, was in fact the *second* of three sons (Nikolai, Ivan, Sergei), and the third died young. 'Uralian' is presumably an error for 'Oryol' in central Russia, some two hundred miles south-west of Moscow, where the Turgenevs lived. But errors like these do not overturn the authority of the obituary, especially since the second of the two might well be a misprint. And the claim that the elder brother of Turgenev met Maria Edgeworth is perhaps confirmed in a reference to 'Mons Turgenief a Russian' in an unpublished letter from Maria to Sophy Ruxton dated 21 March 1831.

There seems no way now of discovering who the author of the article may have been. His account of Turgenev's character and conversation is deeply circumstantial, and its detail carries conviction in itself. One anonymous obituary is all the evidence we have of the most celebrated of all literary debts owed to Maria Edgeworth after that of Scott himself; but it is probably enough.

EXPLANATORY NOTES

ABBREVIATIONS

Butler copy	copy of *Castle Rackrent* (1800), first London edition, with manuscript notes by Maria Edgeworth. See Appendix A in my Oxford English Novels edition, 1964.
ME	Maria Edgeworth (1767–1849).
Memoir (1867)	*A Memoir of Maria Edgeworth, with a Selection from her Letters*. By Mrs. [F. A.] Edgeworth, edited by her Children. 3 vols. (1867) (privately printed).
RLE	Richard Lovell Edgeworth (1744–1817), the novelist's father.
1800 A	*Castle Rackrent*—1st London edition.
1800 B	" 2nd "
1801	" 3rd "
1804	" 4th "
1810	" 5th "
1815	" 6th "
1832	*Tales and Novels by Maria Edgeworth*, 18 vols. (1832–3)—2nd collected edition, revised. Volume i includes *Rackrent*.

(*Title*) (1) RACKRENT] Rackrent is extortionate rent; cf. *The Absentee* (1812): 'It is where there's no jantleman over these under-agents, as here, they do as they plase, and when they have set the land they get rasonable from the head landlords, to poor cratures at a rack-rent, that they can't live and pay the rent . . .' (ch. x).

(2) 1782] The year when ME, at the age of fifteen, settled in Ireland, and also the year of the new constitution establishing the Irish Independency.

Page 1. (3) PREFACE] Evidently written last, probably very late in 1799, and printed last, as the note to the Glossary suggests. The final reference to the Union of Great Britain and Ireland as a foregone conclusion is more difficult to interpret. The Act of Union was not approved by the Irish Parliament, of which RLE was a member, until the spring of 1800, months after *Rackrent* appeared; but it was raised as an immediate political issue in 1798 and actively canvassed throughout 1799. It received the Royal Assent on 2 July 1800, and the Irish Parliament was prorogued for the last time on 2 August. Cf. *Memoirs and Correspondence of Viscount Castlereagh*, vol. iii (1849), pp. 201 f.; and, for an eye-witness account of the last prorogation by a fifteen-year-old, Thomas De Quincey, *Autobiography*, Edinburgh (1853), ch. ix.

Page 2. (4) A plain unvarnished tale] 'I will a round unvarnish'd tale deliver,' *Othello*, I. iii. 90. Cf. p. 96.

Page 3. (5) pointing] pointing of *1801*, &c.

(6) the life of Savage] Samuel Johnson's *An Account of the Life of Mr. Richard Savage* (1744), later included in his *Lives of the English Poets*, had defended the reputation of his dissolute friend, 'a man whose writings entitle him to an eminent rank in the classes of learning'. Margaret Cavendish, Duchess of Newcastle (1624?–74) was the author of a eulogistic biography of her royalist husband, *The Life of William Cavendish* (1667).

(7) The author of the following memoirs] Old Thady, the character representing RLE's steward John Langan, and the only character in the novel who, according to ME's late account, was not imaginary. The transparent fiction that the novel is a 'memoir' edited by ME is maintained with fair consistency throughout, even to a note by the 'Editor' which terminates the novel.

Page 4. (8) Sir Kit] *1801*, &c.; Kitt *1800 A* and *B*. The name is misspelt throughout the 1800 Preface, and in both ways in the text of the novel itself.

Page 5. (9) Squire Western or Parson Trulliber] Western is the hearty Tory squire in Fielding's *Tom Jones* (1749), Trulliber the boorish curate in his *Joseph Andrews* (1742), II. xiv.

(10) of her former existence] *1832* adds '1800' to the end of the Preface.

Page 7. (11) Spencer] Edmund Spenser (1552–99), *A Vewe of the Present State of Ireland* (1596); *Prose Works*, edited by Rudolf Gottfried, Baltimore (1949), lines 1561 f.; for the confusions in Spenser's scholarly references in this passage, cf. ibid., pp. 329 f. Spenser's *Vewe* is later praised in *The Absentee*, where a sensible middle-aged English officer in Dublin recommends to the hero, Lord Colambre, 'the works [on Ireland] which had afforded him most satisfaction; and with discriminative, not superficial celerity, touched on all ancient and modern authors, from Spenser and Davies, to Young and Beaufort' (ch. vi). There is an unexplained note on Spenser on the first fly-leaf of the Butler copy: 'Shooling—law against v. Spenser'.

Page 8, note. (12) in this war] in his warr Spenser, op. cit.

Note. (13) (this should be black bogs)] ME's interpolation.

(14) true and loyal to the family] Butler copy has a note on the first fly-leaf quoting this phrase, with 'write a note on Loyal High Constable'.

Page 9. (15) Moneygawls] Butler copy, *1832*; Castle-moneygawls *1800–15*. The change conforms to p. 42, below.

Page 11. (16) He that goes to bed] The song, which is of unknown authorship, is in its various forms at least as old as the early seventeenth century. Cf. *Rollo : or the Bloody Brother* (1639), a play of the early 1620's by John Fletcher and others:

> And he that will to bed goe sober,
> Falls with the leafe still in October . . . (II. ii);

and Thomas Fuller (1654–1734), *Gnomologia : Adagies and Proverbs* (1732), no. 6219:

> Often drunk, and seldom sober,
> Falls like the Leaves in October.

(17) flocked!] Butler copy; flocked *1800 A*, &c.

(18) it? Just] Butler copy; it, just *1800–15*; it? just *1832*.

(19) villains acted] villains who came to serve acted *1800 A*, &c. The four words are deleted in the Butler copy.

Page 14. (20) herriot] heriot *1800 B*, &c. A payment, often consisting of the best animal, made to the landlord on the death of a tenant.

Page 15. (21) 'learning is better than house or land'] Cf. Samuel Foote (1720–77), *Taste* (1752), an unsuccessful comedy dedicated to RLE's friend Sir Francis Delaval:

> '. . . as the old Saying is,
>
> When House and Land are gone and spent,
> Then Learning is most excellent' (I. i);

or David Garrick, in his prologue to Goldsmith's *She Stoops to Conquer* (1733):

> When ign'rance enters, folly is at hand;
> Learning is better far than house and land.

Page 16, note. (22) Fairy Mounts] Two notes on the first fly-leaf of the Butler copy may refer to this footnote, or to the next. See Appendix A. In an unpublished letter of October 1802, written at Sittingbourne on the way to Dover and Paris, ME wrote to her brother Sneyd: 'Will you beg dear Aunt Mary to look in my bureau for a note about *fairies* for Castle Rackrent. It is written in her own hand—If she finds it she will be so kind to send it to Johnson he is going to publish a *4th Ed of Rackrent*.' The note does not survive. The fourth edition (1804) did not appear for another two years, and then without additional notes.

(23) loy] a narrow spade.

Page 17. (24) that my grandfather heard, before I was born long, under] *1800–15*; that my grandfather heard under *1832*.

Page 20, note. (25) superiors, and tyranny] *1801* (third edition), &c., Butler copy; superiors, any tyranny *1800 A* and *B*.

Page 25. (26) handed her up the steps] *1800 B*, &c., Butler copy; handed her the steps *1800 A*.

Page 26. (27) this heretic Blackamore] his heretic Blackamoor *1804*, &c.

Page 29, note. (28) Lady Cathcart's conjugal imprisonment] The story is told in detail in an obituary of Elizabeth Malyn, Lady Cathcart (1692?–1789) in *The Gentleman's Magazine*, lix (1789), pp. 766–7. She was the widow of the eighth Baron Cathcart (d. 1740), her third husband, when she married Col. Hugh Macguire, an Irish soldier-adventurer and fortune-hunter, in 1745. When she refused to give him her property and jewels he abducted her from their home in Hertfordshire to a castle in Co. Fermanagh, where he kept her confined till his death in 1764, when she returned to England, dying childless in 1789. Mrs. Thrale knew her, and Steele had described her in her nineteenth year in *Tatler*, no. 248 (9 Nov. 1710). Cf. Edward Ford, *Tewin-Water: or the Story of Lady Cathcart*, Enfield (1876). Ford, in an unpublished letter to ME's sister Harriet (Mrs. Richard Butler), suggests that ME may have heard the story from Lady Cathcart's bailiff, 'who had gone over to Ireland to bring her home—this must have been the very man who told Miss Edgeworth in 1800 the wretched state in which he found her'. An unpublished letter of 21 Jan. 1820 from ME to Mrs. Ruxton confirms this. But ME, in her letter to Mrs. Stark of 6 September 1834 (*Memoir* (1867), iii. 152–3), insisted that the resemblance was slight: 'There is a fact mentioned in a note, of Lady Cathcart having been shut up by her husband, Mr. McGuire, in a house in this neighbourhood [i.e. near Edgeworthstown]. So much I knew, but the characters are totally different from what I had heard. Indeed, the real people had been so long dead, that little was known of them. Mr. McGuire had no resemblance, at all events, to my Sir Kit; and I knew nothing of Lady Cathcart but that she was fond of money, and would not give up her diamonds.'

Page 31. (29) 'my pretty Jessica'] *Merchant of Venice*, v. i. 21.

Page 33. (30) aims-ace] ames-ace *1832*, i.e. ambs-ace, a double ace, the lowest possible throw at dice, or next to nothing.

Page 36. (31) vails] tips.

Page 38. (32) CONTINUATION] According to ME's letter to Mrs. Stark of 6 September 1834 (*Memoir* (1867), iii. 153), 'Sir Condy's history was added two years afterwards [i.e. after the composition of the first part of *Rackrent*]: it was not drawn from life, but the good-natured and indolent extravagance were suggested by a relation of mine long since dead.'

Page 39, note. (33) white-headed boy] footnote omitted in *1810*, &c. The use of 'white' as a term of endearment is at least as old as the 15th century; cf. *OED white a* 9. As an Irish colloquialism it may have been influenced by Irish 'bán' (white), which is similarly used.

Page 45. (34) halfpenny] A note on the first fly-leaf of the Butler copy refers to this passage. See Appendix A.

Note. (35) as made me cross myself] Footnote omitted in *1810*, &c.

Page 47. (36) 'Plato, thou reasonest well!'] Addison, *Cato: a Tragedy* (1713), v. i. 1.

(37) 'Angels and ministers of grace, defend us!'] *Hamlet*, I. iv. 39.

Page 50. (38) rate] *1800 B*, &c.; rent *1800 A*.

(39) hoped to find in you 'my father, brother, husband, friend'] hoped to find a—*1800 A*, &c. The addition, which is printed here for the first time, is from the margin of the Butler copy.

Page 53. (40) cut down a tree] A note on the first fly-leaf of the Butler copy probably refers to this passage: 'Tree—kitchen fire.' See Appendix A.

Page 54. (41) writs come down to the Sherriff] Years later, in an unpublished letter to her sister Harriet of 25 April 1825, ME congratulated herself on her picture of Irish judicial corruption: 'The state of our Sherriff-business will astonish the English—They will see that Castle Rackrent was no fable—It is impossible in some cases to color up to the truth—I shd not have dared to have represented Sir Condy or any of his tribe as paying £1500 per annum as hush money fees to the Sherriff or Sub.'

Page 55. (42) not half beds enough] A note on the first fly-leaf of the Butler copy probably refers to this passage: 'No beds for servants—they sleep in the day time.'

Page 56. (43) Gulteeshinnagh] *1810* adds the only new footnote since 1800:

At St. Patrick's meeting, London, March 1806, the Duke of Sussex said, he had the honour of bearing an Irish title, and, with the permission of the company, he should tell them an anecdote of what he had experienced on his travels. When he was at Rome, he went to visit an Irish Seminary, and when they heard who he was, and that he had an Irish title, some of them asked him, 'Please your Royal Highness, since you are an Irish peer, will you tell us if you ever trod upon Irish ground?' When he told them he had not, 'O! then,' said one of the Order, 'you shall soon do so.' They then spread some earth, which had been brought from Ireland, on a marble slab, and made him stand upon it.

(44) by this piece of honesty] The Glossary of *1810*, &c., adds the only new item here:

In a dispute which occurred some years ago in Ireland, between Mr. E. and Mr. M., about the boundaries of a farm, an old tenant of Mr. M.'s cut a *sod* from Mr. E.'s land, and inserted it in a spot prepared for its reception in Mr. M.'s land; so nicely was it inserted, that no eye could detect the junction of the grass. The old man who was to give his evidence as to the property, stood upon the inserted sod when the *viewers* came, and swore that the ground he *then stood upon* belonged to his landlord, Mr. M.

The Editor had flattered himself that the ingenious contrivance which Thady records, and the similar subterfuge of this old Irishman, in the dispute concerning boundaries, were instances of *'cuteness* unparalleled in all but Irish story: an English friend, however, has just mortified the Editor's national vanity by an account of the following custom, which prevails in part of Shropshire. It is discreditable for women to appear abroad after the birth of their children till they have been *churched*. To avoid this reproach and at the same time to enjoy the pleasure of gadding, whenever a woman goes abroad before she has been to church, she takes a tile from the roof of her house, and puts it upon her head: wearing this panoply all the time she pays her visits, her conscience is perfectly at ease; for she can afterwards safely declare to the clergyman, that she 'has never been from under her own roof till she came to be churched'.

Page 59. (45) custodiam] a three-year grant of land made by the Exchequer under Irish law to a lessee.

Page 65. (46) my dear] my *1800 A*, where 'dear' is accidentally printed only as a catchword; corrected *1800 B*, &c.

(47) 'The sorrows of Werter'] Goethe's *Werther* (1774) had been translated into English for the first time, incomplete, by Richard Graves (1779), a version often reprinted before 1800.

Page 71. (48) gripers] extortioners.

Page 72. (49) quit-rent] a rent paid by the occupier in lieu of services rendered.

Page 74. (50) tings] things *1804*, &c.

Page 75. (51) Sarrah] Sorrow, i.e. the Devil, a strong negation. Cf. John Galt, *The Provost*, Edinburgh (1822): 'Without a smith there was no egress, and sorrow a smith was to be had' (ch. v).

Page 77. (52) tink] think *1800 B*, &c.

Page 79, note. (53) childer] footnote omitted in *1832*.

Page 83, note. (54) taplash] washings of casks or glasses; dregs.

Page 87. (55) shawls to] shawls by *1800 A*, corrected by erratum, p. 182.

Page 91. (56) shister] *1832*; sister *1800–15*.

(57) gauger] exciseman, one who gauges the content of a cask.

Page 94, note. (58) tester] a silver coin, from French *teston*, derived from Italian *testa*, a head. Cf. Shakespeare, *2 Henry IV*, III. ii. 296; *Merry Wives*, I. iii. 96.

Page 97. (59) Mr. Young's picture of Ireland] Arthur Young (1741–1820), *A Tour in Ireland* (1780), had described conditions throughout Ireland in 1776–9, before ME settled there.

(60) Union] The Union was debated by the Irish Parliament throughout 1799, and finally approved by George III on 2 July 1800, some six months after the appearance of *Rackrent*.

(61) Warwickshire militia] A number of English militia served in Ireland in the 1790's during the French wars.

(62) to drink whiskey?] *1832* adds '1800' to the end of the postscript.

Page 98. (63) ADVERTISEMENT TO THE ENGLISH READER . . . since it has been printed] The preliminary leaves, i.e. the half-title, title, table of contents, dedication, preface and the like, are normally printed last, so that ME may have shown the printed text of the novel to friends before writing the Preface and Glossary. Because of her hasty decision to add a Glossary at the last moment, and before the novel, the prelims of *1800* were swollen to the exceptional bulk of forty-five pages. The signatures are [ ]^2, a–b^8, c^6.

Page 99. (64) GLOSSARY] In fact a commentary and, as the preceding Advertisement explains, an afterthought, since Thady's narrative was already equipped with footnotes. For the printer's convenience it was printed before the novel in *1800 A* and in the first Irish edition (Dublin, 1800), and assumed its natural place after the novel in *1800 B*, &c.

In an unpublished letter to her cousin, Sophy Ruxton (7 May 1800), written a few months after the novel appeared, ME confessed that one of the notes was by her father: 'has Castle Rackrent ever reached you?—One of the notes in the Glossary is my father's writing.—Guess which it is—if you think it worth while'. Cf. Glossary, note to p. 40, above.

The device of a commentary is exceptional in the eighteenth-century English novel, but not without precedent: Beckford, for example, had furnished his *Vathek* (1787) with one. ME's example was later followed by Scott in some of the Waverley novels, where the commentary became a characteristic of the historical novel.

Page 100. (64a) he was answered by that of the head;] they were answered by that of the foot *1800 A*, corrected in *1800 B*.

Page 103. (65) sixty turkies] thirty turkies *1800*, &c., corrected in the margin of the Butler copy.

Page 108. (66) for want of ready money] for ready money *1800 A*, &c., corrected in the margin of the Butler copy.

(67) Maynooth] Minnouth *1800*, corrected in Butler copy and in *1832*. St. Patrick's College, Maynooth, in Co. Kildare, was founded in 1795 as the chief seminary for Irish priests, who had previously gone abroad to be trained. The chief benefactor was Edmund Burke.

(68) *to dock the entail*] This legal note was perhaps by RLE; cf. 129, above.

terms are] terms *1800 A*, &c., corrected in the margin of the Butler copy.

Page 109. (69) his richer neighbour's] his neighbour's *1800*, &c., corrected in the margin of the Butler copy.

(70) 'Nothing strange—The matter,] 'The matter, *1800 A*, &c., corrected in the margin of the Butler copy.

Page 111. (71) observe, that this custom] observe, this custom *1800 A*, &c., corrected in the margin of the Butler copy. Cf. *Memoirs* (1820), 1. 70.

Page 114. (72) There *Killing is no murder*] *There killing is no murder. 1800–15*, corrected in margin of Butler copy and in *1832*.